P9-CRT-016

The
Promise-Keeper

The Promise-Keeper

by

Muriel Leeson

MOODY PRESS

CHICAGO

© 1975 by
MURIEL LEESON

Originally published as *Oranges and U.F.O.'s*,
by Scholastic-TAB Publications, Ltd.

ISBN: 0-8024-6758-X

1 2 3 4 5 6 7 Printing GB Year 88 87 86 85 84

Printed in the United States of America

Contents

CHAPTER		PAGE
1	Oranges and UFOs	7
2	Promise-Keeper	15
3	Enemy Attack	25
4	The Give-Away Cake	36
5	Land of the Small Ones	44
6	Before and Behind	64
7	Lily McGonigle	70
8	Wieners and Genes	76
9	The White Shields of Abilan	84
10	True Citizens	112

1

Oranges and UFOs

Bill Baker went up the front steps two at a time and slammed into the house, shouting for his brother, Harold. In his mittened right hand he held a snapshot and in his left a seventh-grade textbook and a drugstore film envelope. He kicked off his snowy boots, flung the book and envelope on the davenport, and rushed into the kitchen.

"Harold! Mother! Look at this! A perfect shot of the UFO!" He held out the small black-and-white picture, and Harold, who was just finishing his lunch, reached for it. As he looked at it his eyes grew round with wonder, and his mouth dropped open. It was taken in their back yard in Pillsbury, looking west, and it was without a doubt, the clearest picture of a flying saucer he had ever seen.

"Bill! It really *is* a saucer! I thought you were kidding when you told me you took a picture of one Saturday! *Wow!* How long did it stay? Who else saw it? How low did it come?" Questions poured out like a flood. "Boy, I sure picked a swell weekend to go to Peter's farm."

Before Bill could answer, the front doorbell rang.

That would be Harold's gang calling for him to go out and play in the snow until time to leave for school. They'd forget snowballs in a hurry when they saw the picture. Harold raced to the door and flung it open.

As soon as he was out of earshot, Mrs. Baker whispered to Bill, "The picture's really very good. The thread doesn't show at all. When are you going to tell him the truth?"

Bill was listening to the excited voices at the front door. The picture was absolutely fantastic! Then he realized his mother was speaking and turned to her. "Tell him? Oh—in a day or two. I want to have some fun first. I sure wish it *were* real."

"Did you bring the oranges?" His mother put down the pile of freshly ironed clothes she had just brought up from the family room.

"The what? Oh, the oranges. No, I forgot. I just took one look at that picture, and all I could think of was getting home to show Harold. I went right past the store. I'll get them on the way home after school."

Mrs. Baker sighed. "Bill," she said, "I do wish you could keep your mind on what you're doing." She sorted some underwear and sweat shirts from the pile of clothes and put them on the end of the counter. "Here. When you go upstairs, put these in your drawer."

Upstairs! Bill looked at the clock. It was already 12:30. "Oh-oh," he said, pulling off his parka and cap, "good thing you reminded me! I forgot my math homework for this afternoon. Hooper'll kill me!" He grabbed his textbook, a plate of sandwiches, and a glass of milk, and headed for the stairs. "I'll have to do it while I eat. Never mind the soup."

His mother's voice followed him. She sounded

cross. "Bill Baker! Why don't you just try doing the job at hand? Your head's always full of everything but what you should be doing. You even forgot the clothes! I'll tell you this—whatever *else* they need on the moon, they can do without dumbbells! What would have happened if Armstrong had forgotten to pick up the rocks when he made his moon landing?"

He heard her go back down to the family room, tramping hard the way she did when she was exasperated. It was too bad about the oranges, but she didn't understand. How could a guy think of oranges and underwear and homework when maybe there were *real* saucers up there?

He sat at his desk frowning, aware of the clock ticking on his bureau. He'd never get done in time! He could hear the excited voices of Harold's friends at the front door, making remarks about his UFO picture. He wished he could be there, enjoying it, but Hooper had really chewed him out for forgetting his math last week. He sighed and began the first problem.

By noon the next day not only Harold's friends, who were eight and nine, but most of his own twelve-year-old gang had seen the fake UFO picture and accepted it as real. He had become a celebrity. The thought occurred to him that perhaps he should send the picture to one of the UFO magazines, for fun. Maybe they'd print it!

"Harold," he said, "where's my latest UFO magazine—the one you took to show Peter?"

"In the bedroom."

Mrs. Baker spoke up. "I put all your magazines on the top shelf of your clothes closet. I'm tired of picking them up off the floor." She turned to Bill. "You forgot the oranges again yesterday, and I didn't have time to shop this morning. Now, will you *please* get them today? There isn't one left."

"OK." Bill sighed. Didn't mothers ever think of anything exciting? Who needed oranges? They could skip them for once.

Harold had gone upstairs, and Bill could hear him dragging a chair across the floor over their heads. There was silence and then a sudden crash and a series of thumps. Mother ran to the foot of the stairs.

"Harold? Are you hurt?"

A voice came from the depths of the bedroom closet. "No. I just knocked a bunch of junk down, and then I fell off the chair trying to catch it." There was more noise as Harold began to pick up fallen boxes and books. Finally they heard him come downstairs. Bill looked at the clock. It was too late to get the picture ready to mail now.

Harold's voice cut into his thoughts. "So we have UFOs made here in town, do we? Pretty smart. How did you get it up in the sky?" He was holding the empty "Aurora" UFO model box in one pudgy hand. He looked more disappointed than cross.

Bill stared at the box with the saucer picture on the lid. He should have gone for the magazine himself, but thinking about sending away the snapshot had made him forget he had hidden the empty box on the closet shelf. He sighed. It had been fun while it lasted.

"I made the model while you were at the farm, then tied it to the porch roof overhang to take the picture. I never expected it to turn out so well; I figured I'd fool you for a while though."

Harold grinned. "You sure did. But I wish it had been a real saucer. Where's the model? Can I see it?"

"Sure. It's hidden in my drawer." He looked at the

10

kitchen clock. "I'll show you after school. Don't tell the other kids yet, OK?"

Bill and Harold went upstairs, and opening his second-from-the-top bureau drawer, Bill carefully lifted out his pajamas and underwear. He stared. Then he removed the socks and sweat shirts, just to be sure.

The model wasn't there. In its place was a piece of paper with some crooked printing on it. He picked it up and read it aloud.

We are aware of your Activities.
This afternoon we came for your
model. We are taking it to our
leader. We will return it
when you have obeyed the
following instructions:

−−. −−− .... . −−− −−−
.−−. .−− −−. −−−. . . ..

Bill felt as though he had stepped into a science fiction story. What was going on? Who would use Morse code? Was Morse interplanetary? What about the English printing? He looked at Harold. "Where's the code book? I can't think straight."

His hands were shaking as he began to decipher the message.

GET THE OR—He gasped. Orders? From where? No, it wasn't. It was—ANGES.

Oranges?

Then he remembered—the underwear he hadn't put away yesterday. Mother had no doubt found the model and taken it. He was disappointed, but it *was* funny.

"Harold, Mother wrote it!" He hated to admit it, but for a moment he had really thought—oh well, it was a good joke. They went downstairs.

"OK. Joke's over. Where's my model?"

His mother was smiling. "You get it when I get my oranges."

Fifteen minutes later Bill ran in the back door and thumped a brown paper bag down on the counter. "There! One dozen oranges. Now where's my model?"

"Thank you," Mrs. Baker said, taking the bag. "It's on the top shelf of the linen closet."

Harold had been waiting for him, and they went back upstairs. Bill opened the door of the hall closet and looked up, but there was no model. He got a chair and stood on it, searching every shelf. There were sheets, pillowcases, and towels, but no model.

He yelled downstairs, "Mother! It isn't here. Did you say the *top* shelf?"

"Yes. You can't miss it. After you went back to school this afternoon, I took it from your drawer where I noticed it yesterday. I put it on the top shelf and left the note in its place. It must be there!"

Bill ran his hand across the sheets on the top shelf and even down behind them. It was then that he found the piece of odd material. It was about four inches square and it was neither paper nor cloth, but a sort of silver-gray fiber. As he looked at it, wondering what it was, thin, spidery writing began to appear on it, letter by letter. Very slowly he got down from the chair and handed it to his brother.

"Harold, look at that."

Harold read it, and then they both went back downstairs to the kitchen.

"What kind of trick ink is this?" Bill asked his mother. "Something to do with the warmth of my hand?" But as she took it from him, he realized from the puzzled look on her face that she knew no more about it than they did.

She read it and then sat down suddenly on a kitchen chair, as though her legs wouldn't hold her any more. She looked at them, her eyes staring the way Harold's had when he saw the picture.

"I didn't write it," she said. "Not this one."

"Did Dad?" Harold spoke up.

Mrs. Baker shook her head. "No. There's been no one in the house but me all afternoon. At least, no one you could see." She picked the note up from her lap and read it aloud, her voice a little shaky. It said:

Dear Mrs. Baker:

Thank you for the idea. Our leader really will be interested.

Your friends,
The Small Ones

13

Without speaking, Bill, Harold, and their mother, as if thinking the same thought, went over to the big kitchen window above the sink. They stood there together, staring up into the January sky.

And then they saw it, the shimmering silver disc, just as it vanished into the clouds.

Several weeks passed before it appeared again. By then the Nicodemus Morse Code Club had been formed, with charter members Bill and Harold Baker, Arthur Phillips, Greg Petursson, Kelly Inkster, Patrick O'Keefe, and Jim Taylor. They planned to meet on the last Saturday of each month to practice the code. They had even started to build a clubhouse in a small clearing south of town, though until it was finished they were using Bakers' family room.

In February nothing extraordinary happened. But on March 28—well, only those who attended would ever believe *that* night!

2

Promise-Keeper

Around four-thirty on the afternoon of March 26, Bill completed one more fruitless search through the linen closet. He shook his head as he replaced the last pile of sheets and towels.

"It's not there," he muttered. "It's not anywhere in the house. I keep thinking they might bring it back."

"I take it you mean your saucer model," said his mother.

Bill replied, frowning, "Yes. The kids just won't believe me. They say you and Harold and I only thought we saw the UFO. When I tell them about my model disappearing from the closet and about the note the Small Ones left, they think I'm lying. They say I'm crazy. I told Mr. Hooper, and he said it was very strange, but he didn't really believe me, I know."

Harold spoke up. "They don't believe me, either. Clarence says I ought to be in the funny farm."

Bill wandered into their bedroom, where his mother was putting away clean clothes. He looked at the picture of the model, propped up on his bureau. "The weird part is that they believed *this*," he said. "Until we told them, they thought this was a picture of a real UFO. And it's just a fake. Why did they believe a fake if they won't believe the real thing?"

His mother smiled. "You know why? Because it's a *good* fake. And they saw it with their own eyes. Some people believe only what they see for themselves. Don't forget, you and Harold and I are the only ones who saw the real UFO and read the note."

Bill nodded. "I guess you're right. If only we had shown the note to somebody right away, before it began to disappear. It was gone so fast, and there I stood, holding nothing in my hand. But *we* saw it. Why don't they believe us?"

His mother shut the bureau drawer. "Bill," she said, "people don't accept easily what they can't understand and what can't be proved." She paused a moment, frowning slightly. "However, be that as it may, you and I have to go about our daily affairs and not think so much about it." She looked at the clock. "You have half an hour until dinner. Are you going to start your homework?"

"I guess so." Bill sat down at his desk and picked up a pencil. "Boy, I wish the UFO would come back when the gang was around. I'm tired of having them think I'm nuts."

Harold took some small cars from the cupboard and headed for the stairs. "Clarence says he thinks the whole family's nuts, except Dad. He never saw it."

After his mother and Harold had gone, Bill opened his textbook. He hoped to go into science, and Mr. Hooper had said he'd better work hard at his math. He looked at the first question and tried to concentrate.

Three minutes later he put his pencil down and sat

staring at the snapshot. It *was* good. He had never expected it to turn out so well, and it had been fun fooling the kids. When he had told them about the real UFO and explained that the picture was only a fake, it had come as a shock that they didn't believe him. For two months now he and Harold had talked and talked about it. They had searched the skies morning and night. The gang kept kidding them both; they said the UFO was only a trick of the light. But the note, what about the note? There was no answer for that. He couldn't forget the UFO, and he felt that if it didn't return soon, he really *would* go nuts.

Who were the Small Ones? How could they enter your house unseen and leave again, taking your property with them? The note indicated they were friendly. That was good. It would be pretty awful if they were against you. Who *was* their leader? Would he send them back with the model?

At last he dragged his thoughts back to the math and looked down at the text. But instead of the rows of figures, he once again saw in his imagination the words that had been written on the strange, silver-gray fiber that was neither cloth nor paper:

> Dear Mrs. Baker:
> Thank you for the idea. Our leader really will be interested.
> > Your friends,
> > The Small Ones

Saturday night would be the second meeting of the Nicodemus Club. He would try one last time to convince the gang. One last time.

He picked up his pencil and began again on the

17

math. Tomorrow was Friday, but there was no school. If he got through his homework now, he could have three whole days off! He would have to concentrate.

"Small Ones," he murmured, to no one in particular, "get lost. But if you're planning to come back, how about Saturday night at eight?"

Harold poked his head around the door. He had come upstairs for more cars. "Maybe they'll hear you," he said.

On Saturday everybody turned out for the meeting except Arthur Phillips, who had a cousin visiting for the holiday weekend. His mother said he had to entertain her.

"Too bad Arthur can't come," said Jim. "We could all sit around together and listen to Bill's fairy stories!" He laughed, looking around at the grinning faces.

"Aw, knock it off, Jim." Patrick picked up his pencil. "Let's get on with the code. If Bill's pals turn up, maybe they'll help us. Did you say the note was in code?"

"No!" snapped Bill. "It was in English. Thin, spidery writing on some weird stuff that vanished."

Patrick shook his head. "OK. OK, if you say so. Now how about starting the exercise?"

Bill sat down at the table and put his finger on the sending key. "Ready?" he asked, looking at the five boys who were sprawled about the floor with pencils and notebooks; then he tapped out the first message.

At the end of five minutes he stopped, distracted by Harold who had abandoned his notebook and was arranging his Corgi cars in a circle, their front ends pointing inward. "Harold," said Bill, his finger suspended above the key, "stop fooling with those cars.

If you want to be in the club you have to pay attention. You—"

He stopped abruptly, staring at what a second ago had been an empty circle of blue tile in the center of the ring of cars. Now a small silver disc the size of a bottle cap sat in the middle of the space.

"Harold," he said, "what's that? Where'd it come from?"

Harold shook his head, puzzled. "I don't know. I didn't put it there."

The boys nearest him looked up from their notebooks. Jim, who was closest, called out suddenly, "It's getting larger!"

It was. As they watched, it expanded, pushing the tiny cars aside. Bill jumped up from the table and everyone crowded around Harold.

"What is it?"

"Who put it there?"

"Look at it *grow*!"

It was enlarging itself at an amazing rate. In seconds it was as big as Bill's football—the red hassock—the armchair—the card table—

"What *is* it?" exclaimed Jim. "Look out! It's going to squash us!" His voice was high and squeaky, and he stepped on Kelly's foot as he jumped back.

"I'm scared," said Harold, running behind Bill.

"You guys—get over here!" Bill yelled. Whatever it was, he didn't want to see anyone trapped between it and the walls. Patrick and Greg dashed around from behind it, suddenly aware that the small end of the L-shaped room had neither door nor window through which they could escape. The six boys stood huddled together, all eyes fixed on the shining object which

19

was now the size of the piano—and still growing.

When no more than two feet remained between its silver top and the ceiling, a peculiar sound like the *ping* of a sonar signal came from within. Then silence. It had finally stopped expanding.

"Bill," whispered Harold, "what's going to happen?"

"Shh," Bill answered. "Stay behind me."

He swallowed and waited, every muscle tense. He could see no openings in the smooth expanse of gleaming metal, only the distorted shapes of the family room lights reflected in the upper and lower sections of what looked like an enormous silver yo-yo. Its top, however, was about a foot wider than the bottom, as though some giant toymaker had mismatched two different sizes. It had pushed to the walls any small pieces of furniture in its way and now it sat, silent, motionless, and threatening.

"Why doesn't someone come out?" whispered Kelly.

"Maybe they're already out," said Greg, looking around uneasily. "They could start to grow from nothing too—"

Suddenly, without warning, a small round door on the top of the UFO popped up like a jack-in-the-box lid, and a head emerged, followed by two small hands that grasped the rim of the opening. Before anyone could even gasp there was a flash of gold, and swift as a frog leaps from its hiding place, a small man jumped out to land lightly on the tile floor before them.

He was barely three feet high and dressed in tights of gold cloth, like a circus performer. His hair, which was very short and curly, shone with the same golden glow. He was well formed and moved with the smooth and agile grace of a skilled acrobat. Smiling, he ap-

20

proached them with his right hand extended, palm up.

Bill stared at him, open-mouthed, eyes wide. "But where did you—how—?" His words trailed off as he tried to take in the astounding fact that what had previously happened only in books and comics was now happening to *him*! A visitor from outer space in *his* family room!

"Boy! Did you see that leap!" This was Greg, who considered himself better than average in tumbling. "Does earth have less gravity than your planet, or could you do that anywhere?"

The newcomer looked at him, obviously amused by his reaction. "Anywhere," he said, smiling.

"You speak English!" shouted Kelly. "We can understand you!"

"There would be no point in coming if you couldn't," answered the visitor, reasonably enough.

Pat looked back and forth from the small golden figure to Bill, and at last he spoke, his voice awed.

"You know, we all kidded him about the saucer—and the note," he said. "But you really do exist. Are you the leader?"

"Yes," was the answer, "I am. And I did find the model most interesting." He turned to Bill, leaving the rest to gape and make comments as they pressed around him. "Look, Bill," he said, directing attention to his extended right hand.

There was a sudden silence.

In the center of the pink palm sat an object that resembled a gray coin. As they watched, it began to increase in size until, within seconds, it was recognizable as the missing saucer model.

"Take it," he said, in his soft, pleasant voice. "I

21

decided to return it personally. I understand you are having trouble." As Bill reached out and took the model, the small man gazed at him intently, his sharp eyes, more silver than blue, twinkling and shining like tiny stars. At last he turned to the rest of the group.

"If you are all now convinced that your friend is sane, we will leave. We have business of a similar nature elsewhere." He smiled at them, turned around, and with a second leap re-entered the silver object. His small hand could be seen reaching up to close the door. But before it was halfway down, his face appeared again above the rim of the opening.

"My name is Promise-Keeper," he said. "I will come again." With that he snapped the door into place and at once the craft began to shrink.

"It's going!" cried Bill. "Oh, why doesn't it stay!"

They watched, fascinated, as it continued to decrease in size until there was only a speck on the blue tile floor, and finally nothing at all. The cars once more formed their circle.

Bill looked down at his saucer model, and then at the boys standing around him.

"You see," he said slowly, "I wasn't crazy. I really wasn't."

For a few seconds nobody spoke. At last Greg spoke in a voice that was barely above a whisper. "It's weird. Did we really see that?"

"Certainly. Six of us saw it. We can't *all* be crazy." This was Kelly, who was quiet, but quick-thinking.

Harold ran to the door. "Let's look outside. Maybe we'll see it outside, like before."

They rushed after him upstairs and out into the yard, heedless of the chill March wind, but there was no sign of the silver object, only the quiet sky and the stars. Finally, satisfied that it wasn't there, they headed back into the house.

Then Bill remembered something. "Arthur!" he exclaimed. "Let's phone him!" He could hardly wait to share this latest, stupendous news.

He dialed the number with a finger that trembled with excitement. When Arthur came to the phone Bill began to relate the events of the last half hour while the rest of the gang crowded about trying to hear and yelling their comments into the mouthpiece.

Arthur's voice, when at last it came, was so low that only Bill could hear. He listened intently and then turned to the others, his expression stunned.

"He says he doesn't believe us. He says we're putting him on!"

"Doesn't believe us! Let me talk to him!" Patrick grabbed the phone from Bill and spoke earnestly; and then Jim tried, and Kelly, and finally Greg. But it was no use. Arthur refused to believe them.

Later, when their parents came home, they met more skepticism.

"But Mom, you saw the UFO! You read the note." Bill was appalled.

Mrs. Baker shook her head. "I know. I know. But this—well—well, how do I know you're not fooling? I mean—it's too much!"

Mr. Baker was obviously annoyed. "Listen," he said, "I'm fed up with these Small Ones, whoever they are, and it's about time you packed it up!"

The next morning the whole family went to church. Arthur Phillips's family was in the pew next to the

Bakers, and Bill contrived to sit next to Arthur.

"Arthur," he whispered, "we really saw him, we really did! He was dressed all in gold."

Arthur smiled a very skeptical smile. "Oh yeah, I'm sure. You guys don't fool me. Not twice." He lowered his voice even more when his mother nudged him with her elbow. His words were the merest breath. "When *I* see him, I'll believe you!"

A sharper poke from Mrs. Phillips ended further conversation.

And then, as it was Easter Sunday, Pastor Miller read the resurrection account from John's gospel. When he finished, Bill turned to Harold.

"Harold," he muttered, "now I know what they mean. About being a doubting Thomas. There's one next to me."

Harold popped his head out, his eyes wide with expectation. But all he saw was Arthur Phillips, a thin boy with glasses, staring down at his Sunday shoes.

Later that day, while they were painting plane models in the family room, Harold asked the question that was uppermost in their minds.

"Do you think they'll come back, as Promise-Keeper said?"

Bill stared at the place on the tile floor where the disc had first appeared. Then he remembered something, and all doubt vanished.

"Yes, they'll come. Can't you see? They *want* us to believe. They came for the gang, and they'll come for Arthur."

He picked up his paint brush, satisfied at last and content to wait.

In less than a week, his patience was rewarded.

3

Enemy Attack

They waited in the half-finished clubhouse, sprawled about on the tarp-covered earth floor. In spite of the time and effort they had spent on the hut, it was still far from comfortable. They would have preferred to be outdoors, but the Small Ones had clearly indicated they must wait inside the clubhouse.

It was the night of Thursday, April 2. They were all there, just as the note had directed; and they were trying to describe to Arthur the exact shape of the UFO as they had seen it in Bill's family room on the previous Saturday.

Of the seven boys who made up the group, Arthur was the only one who was perfectly calm. "How long are we going to wait?" he asked, looking out through the old screen door at the swiftly darkening sky. "There's an awful storm coming up."

Bill, who was sitting near him, answered. "The note said they would come at seven o'clock." He looked at his watch. "That's in exactly five minutes."

"This better not be a joke. I didn't come out here to give you guys a laugh."

25

They could hear the wind stirring in the poplar trees along Big McClintock River. It increased and gathered force until the bushes began to bend with the strength of it.

"It's getting very dark," said Kelly, glancing out the door. As he spoke a jagged fork of lightning ripped across the sky in the direction of Humber's farm, which lay beyond the trees on the other side of the highway.

"Why did they want us to come to the clubhouse?" asked Patrick.

"I don't know," Bill answered. "The note just said, 'To the members of the Nicodemus Morse Code Club: Bring Arthur and be in your clubhouse at seven this evening.' It was signed 'The Small Ones.' I found it on my desk when I woke up this morning. I only had time to read it and show it to Harold—then it vanished. It was on the same silvery-gray stuff as before, with the same spidery writing."

"Did your folks see it?"

"No. I didn't even tell them about it."

There was a distant rumble of thunder, and when they looked out again they could see rain, way off in the east beyond Humber's.

"It's seven and they aren't here," said Arthur, getting to his feet. "Joke's over."

"Hold on," said Bill, grabbing him by the leg of his jeans. "Your watch is fast. It's only two minutes to seven."

"*If* they exist, they better make it by seven, or I'm going. Why should I give you guys a laugh and miss my TV program too?" he grumbled, sitting down again.

As they waited they looked through the screen,

26

across the open space to the trees now blending into a dark mass as the gray twilight retreated before the blackness of the night. The clouds were thick, blotting out the moonlight and turning the clearing into an eerie spot full of shadows and dim shapes.

"Look!" yelled Harold. "On the river bank!"

They crowded to the door, peering in the direction of his pointing finger, and then they saw the silver yo-yo-shaped object, glowing and increasing in size as before! It gleamed near the still-leafless bushes, pushing aside dry, brown branches as it expanded. When it reached the size it had been in the room, the same peculiar sonar-like sound came from inside it, and expansion suddenly stopped. The door on the top popped up, and in the gloom they saw the familiar flash of gold.

A second later Promise-Keeper was standing before them in the clearing. They pushed out of the clubhouse and surged toward him.

"We are late," he said. "I am sorry, and we have been followed. They will be here any moment."

Arthur had pushed to the front of the group. "He's real!" he yelled. "He's real! You didn't make him up!"

Promise-Keeper smiled, his silver eyes twinkling and flashing in the shadows. "So at last you believe? We are glad. I—"

The rest of his words were lost as a great sheet of lightning flashed across the clearing, for a moment revealing every bush and tree as clearly as though it were noon. Seconds later a tremendous crash of thunder heralded the arrival of the storm. The rain began, gently at first but rapidly increasing to a torrent.

"*Who* will be here? *Who* followed you?" asked Bill, barely aware of the downpour.

Promise-Keeper looked up into the patch of sky directly above them, then at the trees that surrounded the clearing. "Our enemies. The Dark Ones. They will either land here, as we did, or come out above tree level and attack from overhead. They are very good at hiding in trees, especially at night." He glanced up again and then pointed. "Look!" he said, and the boys crowded around him, staring up into the huge elm behind the clubhouse.

Part way up, like a light in the bare branches, was a tiny orange glow. Without warning it flashed down toward them, and in the second before it hit the clubhouse roof and glanced off to land on the grass, they could see it was a silver arrow with a flaming tip. It lay on the ground, still burning in spite of the rain. Bill started toward it, but Promise-Keeper took his arm with small, cool fingers.

"Don't touch it. The tip is poisoned. It will go out in a moment. It's not your kind of fire, and it won't burn your clubhouse."

There was a yell from Arthur. "Look! In the trees—hundreds of them!"

He was right. The poplars and smaller elms around the clearing were filled with the tiny fires. Then, as the boys stared, wondering how so many could have appeared without their noticing, the attack began. Hundreds of silver, fire-tipped arrows began to pour down into the clearing.

They turned, instinctively seeking shelter in the clubhouse, but Promise-Keeper stopped them.

"That isn't the way. The building won't shield you now that they've seen you. Get in a circle, put the youngest in the middle, and stand as close together as you can."

They did as he directed and huddled into a group with Harold crouched down in the center. Moments later a second shower of arrows descended, and now they began to feel the first touch of the flaming tips on their flesh.

The fiery points were like needle jabs—a quick pain and then nothing. Though the arrows penetrated the toughest denim with ease, they caused no burn on the boys' flesh, no penetration beyond a sixteenth of an inch—just the sudden sharp sting. After the points pricked their flesh, the arrows fell to the grass to lie flaming and harmless.

Promise-Keeper was no longer alone. Leaping out from the open door of the UFO came a score of Small Ones, clad as he was and resembling him in every way. They clustered around him, holding up large oval-shaped white shields to deflect the arrows. The boys noticed that along with his shield each Small One had a golden pouch slung over his shoulder.

"Wait until they come down," they heard Promise-Keeper say. "They're still out of range."

For a few seconds more the silver arrows pelted them, amid the crashing of thunder and the great flashes of lightning that lit up the clearing. Then, with no warning, a hundred or more small creatures descended.

Swooping out of the trees like bats, they landed in a circle around the boys and the Small Ones. They were the same height as the followers of Promise-Keeper, but in no other way did they resemble them. Their garments were black and slimy and hung about them like rotted weeds. There was a horrible stench about these tattered shreds of coverings; even so they were better than the white, grublike flesh that was revealed when the gusts of wind blew them apart. Dull black hair, tangled and wild, hung below the shoulders of these creatures, and their eyes, dark and glistening like the water at the bottom of a well, flashed points of silver light. Their terrible eyes stared out of pasty white faces in which there was no beauty, only the gaunt and vicious expression of creatures riddled with evil and bent on destruction.

Bill felt his knees grow weak, and a shiver passed through his body. "They're awful!" he said, his voice barely audible. "I hate how they watch you."

Harold peeped out from behind Bill's shoulder. "Their hair looks like spider webs!" He was whispering, not wanting to attract the personal attention of a pair of the terrible eyes.

"Shh! Keep down."

There was a quick hand signal from the largest of the batlike group, and then each Dark One reached over his shoulder into what resembled a gray quiver, half hidden among the black coverings. Within seconds more flame-tipped arrows flew toward the boys, hurled like tiny spears with amazing accuracy of aim.

At that moment Promise-Keeper raised his arm.

"Now!" he cried, and at the word his followers reached into their golden pouches and began throwing dozens of white, rectangular-shaped stones at the Dark Ones. Some fell short of their mark, but whenever one hit, a black figure would drop to the ground and begin to disintegrate. Those nearest to the stricken one would stop hurling arrows or, if they continued, would miss their targets.

There was a shriek of rage from the Dark Leader and a final shout as he rallied the remainder of his force. With a last terrible flutter of their rotten garments, they shot up into the blackness of the sky and vanished from sight above the treetops.

Promise-Keeper spoke to his followers. "Enough. They won't be back for a while." He walked over to where the boys huddled, still looking up trying to see where their assailants had gone.

"Are you badly hurt?" he asked.

"No," said Bill. "Those things are like being stuck with needles. They'll need bigger stuff than that for us. But why didn't they shoot at you?" He had realized suddenly that not one silver arrow had been aimed at the Small Ones.

Promise-Keeper smiled. "We had shields. They know nothing penetrates Abilan. Anyway, it was you they were after."

"But why us? What did we do?" Bill asked.

"Yeah—how come?" Other voices joined in, puzzled now that the excitement was over.

"You know that we exist. They hate that. And that is what the poison is for."

"The poison!" Bill had forgotten about it. "Will we be sick from it?"

"Not physically—although you could be if you had enough of it." Promise-Keeper began to examine each boy. "I'm afraid the only one who completely escaped was this young fellow in the middle. Your bodies protected him."

It was then that they noticed a peculiar thing. Although the poison tips had penetrated their jeans and even the leather and canvas of their shoes, they had no power to go through flesh—just to prick it. So wherever the leg or arm or body of one boy had been in front of the body of another, there was no penetration of the protected flesh underneath.

"That's what we call 'lapping,'" said Promise-Keeper. "This is why when you have no shields you must huddle in close to one another, with the biggest on the outside to get the most lapping. By this method the group as a whole absorbs less poison."

"But what does the poison do?" asked Bill.

"It depends on how much you get into your system. Over a certain level and you will find all remembrance of us gone. With less poison you will remember vaguely, but you will think of us as a dream or hallucination. The worst is when you return to the state Arthur was in before he saw us—with no ability to believe we exist at all, unless we return and you see us again."

"Oh, no!" said Bill. "That's awful. Can't you help us? We don't want to forget you. We'd like to go with you in the UFO, if you can fit us in."

The other boys nodded and began to add their pleas to his. "Can't you take us to your world, wherever it is?"

Promise-Keeper shook his head. "That was my hope. We were to take you tonight and get your shields so that you could see our land in safety. But now, after this attack, there will be a delay. You will feel the effect of the poison any moment now."

They stared at the small golden figure and at his shining followers clustered about him. The rain had begun to let up, and at last it stopped.

Patrick, who had been in the outer circle, broke the silence. "I can't see them properly anymore! They're fading away!"

In moments his cry was echoed by the other boys who had stood closest to him where the attack had been heaviest.

"Wait, wait!" Bill called out, desperate to ask a question. "Will you come back? Will you—"

The voice of Promise-Keeper was very faint in the now empty clearing.

"Yes. But you will only remember us when you—"

His voice was lost, trailing away, and silence descended upon the group, broken only by the drip of water from the sodden trees. When they looked at the place where the UFO had sat on the river bank, there was nothing to see but the dry, brown bushes, their branches broken.

They stood searching the sky where a few stars had begun to appear.

"Look!" yelled Harold. "There it is!"

Their eyes followed his pointing finger to a small silver sphere that slipped into the clouds and disappeared.

"They're gone, " said Bill. "They're gone."

"Who's gone?" asked Patrick, a puzzled look on his face.

"The Small Ones. You just *saw* the UFO."

Patrick stared at him. "Are you out of your tree?" he said. "I don't know what you're talking about." He looked around at the group. "Why did we come here tonight anyway? What were we going to do?"

Bill looked at him. "Now that you mention it—why did we?" A vague memory stirred in him. "Weren't we supposed to meet someone?" His mind was sluggish. "Wasn't it—wasn't it that—that gold—oh, I must be dreaming. I don't know. My head feels funny. Let's go home." He turned to the other boys.

"Yeah," said Kelly, "Let's go home."

Harold turned to Arthur, who had been near him in the center of the ring.

"They don't remember what happened! The poison is working, just like Promise-Keeper said. Don't you remember?"

Arthur looked at him. "Harold, you're just nuts."

Bill stared at him. "Arthur," he said, "your face is all covered with tiny black specks."

Arthur took out his handkerchief and wiped himself in what he hoped were the right spots.

"Better?" he asked.

"OK" said Bill. He had switched on his flashlight, and now he shone it on the others. Their faces were unmarked, but their hands were speckled, as were his.

Harold called out suddenly, "You jumped up to see, didn't you Arthur? Now I remember—you jumped up to see better, and they got you in the face. A lot of them! You should have kept your head down."

Arthur just looked at him. "Harold," he said, "I think your mom should take you to a head doctor. I really do."

The boys left the clubhouse and walked slowly across the dark clearing through the wet, dead grass to the opening in the bushes where the path led back to the highway.

"You will only remember us when you . . . Why do those words keep coming into my mind?' Bill asked, puzzled.

"That's what he said. Before he faded. Promise-Keeper." Harold looked hopefully at Bill.

Bill shook his head.

"I can't seem to remember," he said. "I just can't seem to remember."

That night Harold had a nightmare and woke up screaming about terrible black slimy things coming out of the trees. Bill finally let him come into his bed.

"They had white fingers like worms, and they were going to smother me!" Harold whispered. He stopped suddenly, as though listening. Then a relieved sigh escaped him.

"It's all right," he said. "It's all right. Promise-Keeper told me he won't let them come back. I can go in my own bed now." He got out and trotted back to his side of the room and crawled in under the covers.

Bill sat up and looked at him intently. "*Who* told you?" he said, struggling to catch a thought that kept slipping away. "I don't know what you mean."

"It's OK," said Harold, his voice sleepy. "It's OK. They won't get me now."

Bill stared at him in the dim light. Harold had already shut his eyes and was sleeping so peacefully that his brother could hardly believe he had been so terrified a moment before.

After a long while, Bill dozed off too, still trying to capture an idea that continually eluded him.

4

The Give-away Cake

On June 25, which was a Thursday, Bill and Harold came around the back of the house feeling happy for two reasons. They had no homework, and the next day was the school carnival.

Harold saw them first.

"Bill!" he cried, pointing to the flower bed that ran beside the path under the kitchen window. "Someone's pulled up my marigolds! Oh no!" He dropped to his knees on the cement walk, his voice rising to a wail.

His brother knelt down beside him and picked up a once lovely Lemon Drop marigold. "You sure can't enter those in any show," he said, shaking his head. "They're not only pulled up, they're all broken."

The back door of the house opened, and a small red-haired boy of about five came out.

"What'cha doin'?" he asked. "Sayin' your prayers?"

Bill looked up and then jumped to his feet. Although not a tall boy, he was much taller than his questioner.

"Alfie—you did this! You did it, didn't you? You pulled up Harold's flowers, and now he can't enter them in the show tomorrow." Suddenly he gripped the smaller boy by the shoulder. "If you weren't such a runt I'd drive you right through the cement—you little—"

"Bill Baker—come right here, this minute!"

The voice from the kitchen was his mother's, and she sounded cross.

"Come on, Alfie—*this time* you're going to get it!" Bill yanked the chunky boy along the walk into the house, with Harold trailing behind carrying a broken marigold.

"Now what's all this about? Why were you threatening Alfie?"

Bill told her about the flowers.

"That kid," he said, glaring at Alfie, "has only been here since yesterday afternoon and already he's broken two airplane models, let the air out of my bike tires, and ruined Harold's marigolds. And not once did he get punished! Not *once*! And just because no one saw him do it! What kind of a kid is he? Didn't his mother teach him anything?" Bill stopped for breath.

"His mother's in the hospital with his new brother, his Granny's sick, and he's supposed to be visiting here with your Aunt Hilda. It wasn't *his* fault she had to go home three hours after she arrived and leave him here with strangers. He's just a lonely little boy, and there's no proof he did any of those things." Mother turned to Harold. "I'm terribly sorry about the flowers, Harold, I couldn't feel worse. But if no one saw Alfie tear them up, how can I punish him?"

Bill answered her. "You didn't have to see him. No one else would spoil Harold's chances in the show!" He took a step toward Alfie, who darted quickly behind a chair.

"Never did it! Never did it! Never did any of those things!"

Harold spoke for the first time. "Well, if you didn't, somebody did. People don't bust up their own plane models and tear up their own marigolds." He looked down at the ruined flower in his chubby fingers, and a big tear squeezed out from one eye and rolled down his cheek.

Bill turned fiercely on Alfie. "Some day you'll get too smart," he said. He took Harold by the arm. "Come on—let's go outside."

Alfie smirked. "Mrs. Baker," he said, "can I have a piece of that cake?" He pointed to half a spice cake on the counter.

Mrs. Baker looked at him. "Alfie, you're sure you didn't pull up the flowers?"

"Oh no. I wouldn't do that. Can I have some cake?"

"Yes, Alfie. You may always have a piece of cake if it's cut. Just never touch an uncut cake without asking."

Bill looked back from the door. "You touch one of my mother's 'give-away' cakes and you'll *really* catch it. That's a rule in this house."

Harold looked at Alfie wiping sticky fingers on his shirt with one hand and stuffing spice cake into his mouth with the other.

"I sure wish you'd gone to your Granny's," he said as he followed Bill out.

At seven o'clock that night Bill was still thinking about what a pest Alfie had been since he'd arrived with Aunt Hilda, who had come to visit for a week in Pillsbury. They had welcomed him and had planned to take him to see their school. Then Aunt Hilda had

38

got that long distance call and had had to go back for a couple of days. That's when the trouble began. Maybe they shouldn't have yelled at him so much about the planes. Maybe he *had* dropped them accidentally while they were at school. Anyway, bad things kept happening, though Alfie never admitted doing any of them. And since their mother never punished them unless she was sure, he just went from one thing to another.

They were mending their planes in the family room, and Alfie was fooling around on the floor with some cars when Harold said, "There's no more glue in this tube."

Bill got up. "Keep an eye on you-know-who, and I'll see if there's anything in Dad's cupboard we can use."

He went out of the room and across the basement to the big walk-in cupboard where Mr. Baker kept his supplies. He reached up and put on the light and then he stopped, his hand still on the switch.

Sitting on the top shelf among packages of putty, cans of paint, and the turpentine bottle was something that didn't belong there at all: a great big three-layer chocolate cake in a transparent plastic cake-saver.

Bill stared it. It was probably for tomorrow. Mom always made chocolate cake for the carnival—but what was it doing up there? She knew he and Harold never touched her give-away cakes. There was no need to hide it in Dad's cupboard.

Suddenly the truth dawned. *Alfie*.

Mother was making sure Alfie didn't touch it. She didn't trust him any more than they did. But she had never punished him because there was no proof. And that wasn't fair. He thought of the broken planes and Harold's ruined flowers.

An idea began to form in his mind—not a very nice

idea, but something had to be done about Alfie. He climbed up on a box and carefully lifted the cake down to the lowest shelf. Then he got a putty knife from the tool box and placed it next to the cake.

"Now, Mr. Smart-Alfie," he said to himself, "let's see you get out of this one."

He took down some of his father's glue and went back to the family room. While pretending to help Harold use it he whispered into his ear. After a few minutes he said to Alfie, "Alfie—put this back in the big cupboard, will you?"

"Why should I?" Alfie looked up, his face saucy.

"Why shouldn't you? That's the least you can do. Here."

Alfie shrugged. He took the glue and went out of the room.

Bill and Harold sat very still, waiting. Alfie didn't come back for quite a while, and Bill almost laughed. He had fallen for it!

"How will Mum know *he* did it?" whispered Harold.

"Because he's such a sloppy kid he's sure to get some on his shirt."

They paid no attention to Alfie when he returned, but later that night, when the little boy was in bed, Bill went down and peeked in the cupboard. There was a big slice gone from the cake.

"Boy, will Mum be sore when she finds *that*." Bill didn't feel too proud of himself, but somebody had to stop Alfie.

Bill was awakened next morning by the sound of Alfie crying and moaning, "Oh, I itch, I itch. Oh, I shouldn't have eaten it. Oh, oh!"

He heard his mother come upstairs and go into the

guest room. There was some whispered conversation and then she came running out, saying in a terribly excited voice, "Oh dear, he ate the chocolate cake! However did he get it?"

Still half asleep, Bill heard her go downstairs and dial the phone and then in a few minutes come back again. Rubbing his eyes and wondering what was going on, he got out of bed and went across the hall. Harold, who was also awake by then, followed him.

Mrs. Baker was sitting on the bed beside Alfie, dabbing what looked like calamine lotion on his arms and chest. Alfie, wearing only his blue pajama pants, was an awful sight. He was covered in a puffy sort of rash, and his face was blotched and tear-stained. Mother turned to Bill. "He ate some of the chocolate cake. How did he find it?"

"Why is he itchy?" Bill asked, avoiding the question.

"He's allergic to chocolate. Aunt Hilda warned me, though she told me he was very sensible about refusing it. But just to be sure, I hid the cake. He loves chocolate, and I didn't want to tempt him. If the swelling had come in his throat he might have choked. How on earth did he find it in Dad's cupboard?"

"Choked!" Bill stared at Alfie, horrified. "I never meant to do *that* to him. I only wanted him to be punished."

Mother looked puzzled. "But Alfie said he took the cake himself—no one gave it to him."

Bill looked at the floor. "I just made it easy for him to find it." He told her the whole miserable story, and finally he turned to Alfie.

"I'm awfully sorry. I didn't know you were allergic. I wouldn't have done that to you!"

Alfie stopped crying and stared at Bill.

41

"Why aren't you glad? Don't you hate me?" He sniffed. "Nobody likes me. They're even getting a new baby at our house. They're tired of me. My mom's gone away to get it, and that's why I'm here." He began to cry again.

Bill felt wretched.

"Alfie," he said, "don't be a dope. Nobody hates you. Well, not now anyway. Look, if you feel better tomorrow I'll buy you a model plane, and Harold and I will help you make it." He turned to his mother, remembering the ruined cake. "You'd better punish me for the cake." It was the least he could do for Alfie.

His mother looked at him for a moment and then she said an odd thing. "Never mind. You don't punish a fellow twice."

Harold leaned over the bed to get a better look at the rash. "Alfie," he said, "that sure was a 'give-away' cake!"

They all laughed then, even Alfie.

The next day Bill and Harold went to the hardware store and bought a beautiful silver Star Fighter. Their mother had offered to help pay for it, but Bill wanted to do it himself. As he pushed the three dollars across the counter he experienced a peculiar satisfaction. Having a silver plane model wouldn't stop Alfie from itching, but it would sure give him something else to think about.

As he left the store, something small and golden rose in his mind, like a light glowing within his thoughts. He felt happy again, as though he hadn't a care in the world. He began to whistle and even to look forward to helping Alfie with the plane.

"I will come in one month."

"Harold, did you say something?" Bill looked down at his brother. It hadn't sounded like Harold's voice, but who else was around?

"Nope." Harold grinned at him. "You must be hearing things."

"Maybe. But I was sure someone said, 'I will come in one month.' "

Harold stopped walking and turned to him, eyes shining. "Maybe you heard Promise-Keeper!"

"Who?" asked Bill, wondering why the name seemed vaguely familiar.

"Promise-Keeper! Can't you remember?" Harold grabbed his arm. "Think hard."

Bill stood on the sidewalk in the June sunshine staring at the model box in his hand but not seeing it, trying to visualize somebody by that name.

"He's small, and dressed in gold—" Harold began.

"It's no good," said Bill. "I can't picture a guy like that. Between you imagining things and me hearing voices—maybe we're both nuts!"

"In a month you'll know," remarked Harold.

5

Land of the Small Ones

On Saturday July 25, Bill sat up and looked across the bedroom at Harold, who had just awakened. He stared sleepily at the brightly painted models on the pegboard over his brother's bed and was reminded suddenly of one not on display, the one they had made for Alfie.

"Alfie sure got a bang out of that silver plane," he said, yawning. "He was a real terror before he got it, but afterward he was OK. I guess his nose was really out of joint because of the new baby." It was a phrase he had heard his mother use. He sat hunched up, elbows on knees, chin on hands, thinking how awful Alfie had looked with his face swollen. Poor little kid. Being allergic to chocolate was rotten. Well, that had been a month ago, and he had done what he could to make it up to him.

His attention was caught by Harold, who had rolled over to face him and was now pointing at something, his eyes wide open.

"Bill, look! There's something on your pillow—behind you!"

Bill whirled around, almost upsetting the tiny golden figure standing in the hollow where his head had so recently lain.

"Promise-Keeper!" he exclaimed, recognizing him at once. It was as though a curtain in his mind had suddenly drawn back, allowing him to recall clearly all the forgotten events connected with the UFO and its owner. "I haven't been able to remember you," he said. "Where did you come from?"

"Out of your thoughts, really." The little figure, no taller than a pencil, jumped to the floor and before their eyes grew to his normal three-foot size.

"That's better" said Bill, wondering where in his thoughts Promise-Keeper could have been. "I might have squashed you the other way," he added out loud.

The golden figure smiled. "Hardly." He looked over at Harold, now completely awake and kneeling on his bed. "You never did forget me, did you?"

"No," said Harold. "But then the arrows never touched me."

"None of you would have been hurt if you had had your shields. I will get them for you tonight."

"Tonight!" they said together, like a chorus. "Where—how—"

Promise-Keeper smiled. "At midnight I will come and take you to our world. It will be necessary to shrink you a little, to fit our—'saucer,' as you call it."

"To *your world*!" cried Bill. "Just us?"

"Yes. Unfortunately the others still can't remember. They wouldn't be able to see me even if I appeared."

"How is it we can see you?" Bill was puzzled. "I had trouble remembering too. It was like thinking of a dream. Just snatches of things, or feelings. How did you know I would be able to see you?"

45

Promise-Keeper motioned toward Harold. "Your brother's memory of me has helped you. You are together a lot. That's all I can tell you—the rest you must come to understand for yourself." He looked at them both. "Don't forget. Midnight. Sleep well until then."

"Sleep!" cried Harold. "How will I sleep? Right now my head's bursting with questions!"

Promise-Keeper laughed, a sound like the ringing of a thousand tiny bells. Then, without warning, he vanished.

Bill stared at the spot on the floor where the golden man had stood. He looked over at Harold.

"Did it happen? Did *you* see him and hear him?"

"Yep. He was there. Boy, are we going to have fun tonight!"

"I hope he comes," said Bill.

Harold stared at him. "Why wouldn't he? Why tell us he was coming if he wasn't? I mean, what would he do that for?"

Bill grinned. "Harold," he said, "you're so right. For a little kid, you sure are exceptional."

Somehow they lived through the day, which seemed a week long. They went to bed, but they couldn't sleep, and at eleven-thirty they got up and dressed again.

At midnight there was a low, rustling noise, and then they saw him, standing between the beds as before.

"I see you are ready to leave. Good." He paused a moment, apparently listening. "Now shut your eyes and keep them shut until I tell you to open them," he ordered at last, in a surprisingly stern voice.

46

They obeyed, wondering what was going to happen. There was silence.

"Harold!" whispered Bill, eyes still shut. "Are you there? I feel as though the bed was gone, but I don't think I'm on the floor—"

"Don't open your eyes, or you will be," came the stern voice of Promise-Keeper.

"I can't feel the bedspread—I think I'm in the air." Harold's voice sounded very close.

"It won't be long," said Promise-Keeper.

They could hear the ticking of the clock on the bureau.

"Now! Open your eyes."

They looked about, astonished. They were both no taller than Promise-Keeper, and they were with him inside the silver sphere that was flattened top and bottom like a yo-yo.

"We're in it!" cried Bill. "We're in the UFO!"

Promise-Keeper nodded. "That's right. And in a short time you will be in our world."

"Look!" said Harold. "You can see out!"

Bill followed his gaze and discovered the window.

In the floor of the upper section, in which they stood, was a circular window directly in line with an identical opening in the lower half. Through these they could see the earth, small, but with the North American continent still clearly visible. Within seconds, as they watched, it shrank to the size of a pea and then vanished from sight, lost in blackness.

"Where are the instruments?" Bill had suddenly realized that the inside of the sphere was a completely smooth sheet of silver-colored metal, except for the small window that allowed them to see below.

47

"We don't need instruments."

"How do you know where you are going when you can only see behind you?"

"The way is well marked."

"What about fuel? Is it down there?" Bill motioned toward the bottom section.

Promise-Keeper smiled. "No," he said. "The upper part *is* the fuel—it lifts and directs the lower part."

"Is the lower part empty?"

"No. It contains all the mechanism to make the craft, and us, visible or invisible to you." He turned back to them.

"We are there," he said. "Please shut your eyes."

They did as he said, resisting the temptation to peek. There was a slight jarring motion.

"Now open them."

They obeyed and found they were again outside the UFO. The darkness had changed to a warm golden light. They were standing on bright green grass in what appeared to be a large garden, where trees covered in bloom and flowers of every description surrounded them. Bill bent down to look at a crimson rose at his feet and found it more beautiful than any he had ever seen on earth.

"Look!" cried Harold. "My marigolds!" Bill followed his pointing finger and saw a long narrow bed of earth containing a row of Lemon Drop marigolds. The stems were sturdy and unbroken, the leaves fresh and green, and each plant bore perfect bright yellow flowers.

Harold ran across the grass and fell down upon his knees to examine them more closely.

"My marigolds!" he cried. "My Lemon Drop marigolds!" He reached out and touched one carefully with his finger, feasting his eyes on its color and sniffing the sharp scent. "Every one back in place!" He sat back on his heels, shaking his head. "I can't believe it," he said. "I just can't believe it!" He looked up at Promise-Keeper, who was standing by his side. "How did they get like they were before Alfie wrecked them? Who made them come alive again?" he asked.

Promise-Keeper was regarding him with a very gentle expression. "They were taken to"—he paused—"to One-Who-Lives-Forever," he finished. "They are part of our Restoration Program."

Harold looked back at the flowers, so beautiful and healthy. "Would you thank that—that 'forever' one for me?" he said at last. "I grew them from seeds—every one."

It was at that moment that he noticed the little brown stick with the ribbon. It was poked into the earth at the end of the row, almost hidden behind the last plant. He reached over and carefully moved the leaves so that he could read the gold printing on the blue satin.

"It says 'First Prize'!" he shouted. "My marigolds won first prize!" He stopped and turned to Promise-Keeper. "But how could that be?" he asked. "I didn't enter them in the show—how could I win?"

The silver-blue eyes of Promise-Keeper twinkled with delight. "If they *had* been entered, they *would* have won," he said. "They were much better than Stinky Smith's carnations—and his were very good, as you know. We felt you were entitled to a ribbon—a prize for what should have been. You did a fine job of caring for them, Harold."

"You better believe it." Bill grinned. "He never

missed a day of weeding or watering. Mom says he has a real green thumb."

Harold looked at his thumb and then back at Promise-Keeper. "With Alfies around, thumbs aren't enough," he said. "You need a—Restoration Program. All the time!" he added, grinning. "I'm sure glad you have one."

"So are we," Promise-Keeper replied. He waited a few moments while Harold continued to examine his flowers. "Now," he urged, when the boy finally got to his feet, "come and try your Slip-Throughs."

"Slip-Throughs?" asked Bill. "What are those?"

"We'll go to Stump Lake where the Small Ones play, and you can see for yourself," Promise-Keeper replied.

He led the way across the clearing into a thick, bushy area. Within a few minutes the narrow path which they followed brought them out to the shore of a tiny lake, hidden away like a bright blue jewel in a setting of green shrubs and trees. Its beauty was marred only by the unusually large number of brown tree stumps that protruded from its surface, not only along the edges, but all across the lake.

"It must be quite shallow," observed Bill. What kind of games could the Small Ones play in such a place?

As if in answer to his thoughts Promise-Keeper pointed to what had hitherto escaped his notice. At the left end of the strip of beach were a dozen or more small silver canoes, each tied with a silver chain to a stump at the lake edge. They were smaller than earth canoes, and there were no paddles visible.

"Those are Slip-Throughs," explained Promise-Keeper, motioning them to follow him. "You may each have one. I will show you how to use them."

"Boy, that will be great!" said Harold, running ahead. "At home they never let me in a boat alone!" The same thought had occurred to Bill, who was used to taking care of Harold, but he felt Promise-Keeper surely knew what he was doing.

When they reached the nearest of the boats, Bill noticed that although they were shaped like canoes each had a small steering wheel and a tiny instrument panel.

"Are they motor boats?" he asked, although there were no motors visible.

"No, in that they are not like yours; yes, in that the power to move is supplied for you," answered Promise-Keeper. He leaped nimbly onto the seat of the second from the end and waited while they climbed into those on either side of him.

"Now," he said, "the steering wheel is no problem, but the three levers will be strange to you."

"They look like popsicle sticks!" cried Harold. "Blue, brown, and silver!"

They saw that above the blue lever was printed in black letters the word *Go*, above the brown *Stop*, and above the silver *Slip-Through*.

" 'Stop' and 'Go' I understand," said Bill, "but what's with this 'Slip-Through'?"

"I'll show you," said Promise-Keeper. "See that big stump?" He pointed along the lake edge to a huge brown stump protruding from the water a hundred feet from shore. "Now watch," he said, pulling the Go lever part way down the slot.

He began to move out across the lake until he was about two hundred feet from the stump. He waved to Bill and Harold and then, to their utter astonishment, began to bear down upon it at top speed!

"Hey! You'll crack up!" yelled Bill, horrified.

"Boy, I hate to watch!" groaned Harold.

The gap was less than six feet.

"Wow! Look at that!" exclaimed Bill, hardly believing his eyes.

At the precise second when the tip of the silver prow was a hair's breadth from the stump, they saw Promise-Keeper reach forward and pull a lever. To their amazement, there was no tearing crash of metal on wood. Still visible, both Promise-Keeper and the canoe glided right through the stump and emerged unharmed on the other side!

As he sped across the tiny lake they heard his laugh like a thousand silver bells ringing out across the sparkling water. In a few minutes he swung around and came back to shore. He sat grinning at them.

"What did you think of that?" he asked, his eyes twinkling and flashing.

"I thought you were a goner!" cried Bill. "Was that the Slip-Through lever you pulled?"

"Yes," replied Promise-Keeper. "Pulling it down all the way changes the nature of both the material in the canoe and us so that, as you saw, we can go through any solid obstacle. Be sure to use the Slip-Through, however. If you start getting scared and avoiding the stumps, eventually the Slip-Through may not work. To retain its power, it must be constantly exercised."

"But that means you need never have a crash—never get hurt by anything—as long as you see the obstacle in time," Bill spoke slowly, but with obvious excitement. "Why, you could go as fast as you liked, as long as you kept watching for stumps and rocks—" He was thinking out loud, seeing the tremendous possibilities. Imagine shooting rapids in a Slip-Through! He had never had this exciting experience in an ordinary canoe, but he had always dreamed of it.

"There is one thing you must remember," warned Promise-Keeper. "Never pull the lever until the very last second. If you use it too soon, you will become solid before you are quite through and very likely will tip over. But you won't come to harm."

"OK, if you say so!" cried Bill. "Come on, Harold— let's try them out!"

"You go first," said Harold. "I'll watch how you do it."

Bill pulled the Go lever and began to move out across the water. Since the speed could be regulated by the position of the lever, he decided that for his first attempt he would approach the stump slowly. He looked across the lake and set his course for the same stump Promise-Keeper had used.

"Go as fast as you like!" called Promise-Keeper.

Bill hesitated only a second and then pushed the blue lever to the bottom of the slot. He leaned forward and felt excitement mount within him. The canoe dashed through the water, and he could see the brown stump coming on, getting larger and nearer.

His heart was beating wildly, and it took all his courage not to swerve to one side. A few feet away from the stump he tightened his grip on the Slip-Through lever.

Now!

He pulled it down, holding his breath, every muscle tensed for a crash.

He had a sense of wind rushing past and saw, incredibly, the silver prow of the canoe slice through the wooden stump like a knife through butter. He sat watching brown going by his legs: now he was in the middle of the stump—now he was past—past—he was through! The stump lay solid and untouched, a foot behind the canoe!

He turned the wheel and came back to shore to a wildly cheering Harold.

"I did it! I did it!" he heard himself yelling. "I got through!"

"I want to try!" Harold cried, beginning at once to head out across the lake.

"Well done," said Promise-Keeper, as he and Bill sat in their canoes watching the younger boy.

"Are you sure he won't get hurt? He can't swim!" Bill was suddenly horrified. In all the excitement he had forgotten!

Promise-Keeper looked at him, his expression grave.

"Would I let him go if it would harm him?" he asked.

Bill shook his head. "No," he said. "Of course you wouldn't. It's just that—well—"

"Watch," said Promise-Keeper. "Because he's nervous he will probably pull the lever too soon, but I promise you he won't be hurt."

He was right. Harold reached forward when he was still a foot away from the stump. They saw him pass about two-thirds of the way through, and then there was a jar and the canoe tipped sideways and spilled him out into the water. Bill jumped up, nearly upsetting himself, but to his amazement Harold seemed quite at home, splashing about beside the stump and reaching for the silver craft with one chubby hand.

"He'll never get back in!" Bill sat down and reached for his Go lever.

"Yes, he will," said Promise-Keeper.

And he did. To Bill's utter surprise, Harold seemed able to lift himself out of the water with ease. He hopped back into his canoe with no more trouble than if he had been on shore.

"How did he do that?" Bill asked. "You'd think the water was holding him up like a floor!"

"It was," said Promise-Keeper. "That always happens after a spill. Nobody drowns here."

Bill relaxed in his seat and waited for Harold to try again. This time, to his great delight, he managed successfully and came back to shore all smiles.

"Wait till the folks hear about this!" he cried.

Promise-Keeper smiled. "Just don't try to give them a demonstration," he said. "Abide by water safety rules on Earth. Remember, things work differently here."

"You better believe it!" agreed Bill, grinning.

The land of the Small Ones was full of amazing reverses. And every one, so far, had been good.

"Now," said Promise-Keeper, leaping out of his Slip-Through, "I must go for your shields. Remember, stay inside the garden. Even here it is not completely safe to be without shields. Outside, the danger is enormous. You *must* wait until I come back. Do you understand?"

"Oh yes," replied Bill. "We won't go away. But how can we tell when we are at the edge of the garden?"

Promise-Keeper directed his attention to a six-foot hedge at the extreme end of the beach, beyond the farthest Slip-Through. "See that?" he asked. "Only on the boundaries of the garden will you find that particular bush. Never attempt to take a path through it unless you have shields—and for the present, I would like to be with you."

"May we use the Slip-Throughs while you are away?" asked Harold.

"You had best wait for me," suggested Promise-Keeper. "After I get your shields I will call for some of the Small Ones, and we will show you how to play our Stump Lake games."

"That will be great," said Bill. "We'll just look around on shore until you come back."

Promise-Keeper smiled. "Very good," he remarked, and began to walk in the direction of the hedge.

After he vanished into its green depths they got out of the Slip-Throughs and began to wander about, examining the various types of flowers and shrubs around the lake area.

Not more than ten minutes had passed when they looked up and saw that he was already back, standing in front of the hedge at a spot a few yards from where he had disappeared from their sight. He waved to them, motioning them to come.

"You didn't bring the shields," said Harold, who had been looking forward to seeing them.

The golden figure frowned slightly and then shrugged. "They weren't ready. I decided to pick them up on the way. We haven't much time."

"You said you would bring them," persisted Harold, who was hard to move when once he had fixed his mind on something.

"Harold, if Promise-Keeper says we'll pick them up on the way, then that's what we'll do!" Bill spoke sharply.

"Come now. I have something to show you more

56

to your taste than flowers and shrubs and even Slip-Throughs! I've decided to take you to the Valley of the UFOs!" The golden figure turned and began to walk away from them.

"The Valley of the UFOs!" cried Bill and Harold together, all thoughts of Slip-Throughs and Stump Lake games pushed from their minds.

With no further discussion they began to follow Promise-Keeper along the path through the hedge. After a few minutes they came out on the other side to find they were in a very dark and deep woods.

Here the trees were tall and so close together that the sky seemed a network of little blue patches, far above them. Golden pencils of light penetrated the gloom of the heavy underbrush through which the path wound.

Promise-Keeper turned to look at them over his shoulder. "We are nearly there. Just wait until you see the valley," he said.

Encouraged, they hurried along, Harold in front. It was very quiet in the woods, and it suddenly occurred to Bill that he had not seen one bird, or heard the chatter of a squirrel in the ten minutes they had been walking.

"Do you not have birds and squirrels here, like we saw in the garden?" he asked.

"Oh, yes."

"They must be hiding, then," said Harold, peering up into the trees that bordered the path.

Promise-Keeper smiled. "Perhaps they are."

"Maybe they're afraid of us," suggested Bill.

"That's it. They are afraid of you. There," he added, as they finally emerged from the silent woods, "how do you like *that* for a view?"

They stood in a grassy clearing overlooking a deep, wide valley. Its slopes were covered with trees and looked quite normal. But far below, the floor of the valley shone and glittered with hundreds of silver objects.

"Take your pick," said Promise-Keeper, flinging his arm out to embrace the whole range of the valley. "Whichever you want you may have for your very own."

"A silver saucer like yours? You mean we can have any one we like—to *keep*?"

Bill felt it was all too good to be true. He and Harold stood looking out across the great expanse of silver UFOs. Any one they liked! How would they ever decide?

As far as he could tell, each saucer was shaped like the one in which they had come, but at the end of the valley closest to where they stood were three much larger than the rest, even allowing for the natural decrease in size of those in the distance.

"There must be thousands of them!" declared Bill.

"It's like being in a yo-yo factory," said Harold, who was practical if not poetic.

Bill let his eyes run slowly over the sparkling UFOs. They stood closely packed, with only a narrow ring of grass separating each one from its neighbor. Trees and shrubs encircled the valley, fading to a narrow dark-green border in the distance.

"I don't know which to choose," mused Bill. "Maybe—"

"Can I come in yours?" Harold broke in. "I'm scared to go alone."

Bill turned to Promise-Keeper. "Can we go together in a big one?" he asked. "Are they all the same inside?"

"Yes, just the same. But make up your mind quickly. There isn't much time."

Still they hesitated, too overawed to move. Questions filled Bill's mind. What would it be like, going alone through space? Could they really get back to earth without help?

The voice of Promise-Keeper interrupted his thoughts. "In a few moments they will all vanish from your sight," he urged. "You *must* hurry!"

"Vanish!" they both cried, horrified.

"Quick, let's take the big one—the one nearest us!" exclaimed Bill, desperate at the thought of losing their great chance. "OK, Harold?"

"Sure!"

Bill turned quickly to the golden figure beside them. "Where's the path down?"

Promise-Keeper smiled. "You don't need a path. Just shut your eyes, think of the saucer and jump. When you open them, you will be inside it."

"Are you sure?" asked Harold. "How do we know?"

"Yes," agreed Bill. "There's a drop of—well, hundreds and hundreds of feet. How do we know we won't be killed?"

"Because I say so. Now, do you want the saucer or don't you?"

Bill and Harold looked at him, then at one another.

"OK," said Bill. "Harold, take my hand. We'll run together."

"Remember, shut your eyes when you jump and don't open them until you are in the saucer."

Bill stopped a moment. "When we get in the saucer, how will we know how to work it? Can we take it back to our world?"

"Yes. There will be instructions inside for you. Now just run together and jump, as I tell you."

"Well, here goes," declared Bill, trying to overcome his fear. "Come on, Harold!"

They joined hands and began to run toward the edge of the cliff. When Bill turned for a last glimpse of Promise-Keeper, his foot caught on something and he stumbled, dragging Harold to the ground with him.

As he scrambled to his feet he saw that he had stubbed his toe on a pile of white, rectangular-shaped stones hidden in a clump of coarse grass. He paused a moment and picked one up. It looked like one of the stones the Small Ones had hurled at their enemies the night of the storm. There seemed to be faint scratchings, like writing, on its surface and he was about to try to read it when Promise-Keeper called out, "Never mind that! You must jump quickly or it will be too late! You can't have a saucer at all if you don't hurry! Jump! Jump!"

Bill looked back at the golden figure, and for the first time noticed something.

"Your—eyes—" he began.

"Jump!" screamed Promise-Keeper. "You will be too late! *Jump!*"

Harold tugged at Bill's hand. "Come on!" he begged. "We have to do as he says or we won't get a saucer!"

"OK," murmured Bill. "I guess it's all right."

They ran forward then, shut their eyes, and leaped out into the valley. As they began to fall, they heard a wild shriek of laughter coming from the top of the cliff.

They dropped straight down, eyes shut, trying to think of the saucer. Down. . .down. . .down. . .until at last their feet touched a solid surface and they realized they had landed unhurt.

"We made it!" cried Bill. "We're in the saucer!"

He opened his eyes. He was still holding Harold's chubby hand.

"Harold"—his voice sank with disappointment—"look where we are!"

Harold opened his eyes and let out a groan.

"At home!" he wailed. "At home in our own room!"

And that is where they were, standing between the two beds on the rug from which they had begun their trip.

"But why would Promise-Keeper do that?" Harold looked puzzled.

Bill turned to look at his brother. "Harold," he asked, "did you see his eyes just before we jumped?"

"No," said Harold. "I was looking at the saucers. I didn't bother much looking at him. What about his eyes?"

"They were black, with points of light in them. Promise-Keeper didn't have eyes like that. I don't think it was Promise-Keeper!"

"He never brought the shields, either," Harold pointed out, remembering. "I wanted to see them."

It all seemed so plain, thinking back. Why would Promise-Keeper tell them they mustn't leave the garden without shields and then tell them they would pick them up on the way?

"What's in your hand, Bill?"

Bill looked down at his right hand and realized he was still holding one of the rectangular white stones.

"I remember—I tripped over a pile of them. I was just going to take a better look when he yelled to jump

61

or it would be too late." He took the gleaming, smooth stone over to his desk and switched on the lamp. Now he could make out the spidery writing that had appeared as scratchings before. "Harold, listen to this!" He read softly, his voice shaky with excitement. "It says, *A true Small One, when touched with this, will remain gold. If, however, the gold be false, and the wearer a Dark One in disguise, where the stone touches a black stain will appear. The imposter thus touched will soon disintegrate.*"

Bill looked at Harold. "Now I know why he hurried us. That was the Dark Leader! He knew if we read this we would find him out. Oh, why were we in such a hurry?" Bill sighed. "I flubbed it."

"No, you didn't," Harold contradicted. "I hurried us, remember? You would have waited. But he said we wouldn't get a saucer if we didn't hurry."

"It's not your fault," Bill protested. "He's a liar, and he fooled us both."

Half an hour later they were still discussing what had happened. Bill had gradually begun to realize something.

"Harold," he exclaimed, "it's not as bad as before! This time we are still remembering! We are back here, but we can remember the UFOs and the Slip-Throughs—and everything we did! The Dark One wasn't able to take that away!"

Harold grinned. "He was so busy trying to keep us from reading the stone that he forgot to shoot at us! He outsmarted himself, I guess."

Bill began to feel better. "Well, now we have to wait again and hope Promise-Keeper will come back and give us another chance. If there is a next time, I hope we don't mess it up." Bill shook his head, thinking of all they must have missed by their sudden return.

"Next time," said Harold, "we'll take the stone with us. After we touch Promise-Keeper with it," he added.

"Right," agreed Bill. "*Next* time."

It was later, just as they were falling asleep, that an unhappy thought occurred to him. "Harold," he whispered, turning toward his brother's bed, "I was just wondering if the Dark Ones could ever put so much poison in us that we would *never* remember Promise-Keeper and never be able to see him again."

"I don't know." Harold's voice was very low. "I think that's what they really want. Maybe they could even make it so we couldn't ever get home again. Remember, Promise-Keeper said the danger was enormous without the shields. If you hadn't tripped over the stones, maybe the Dark One would have shot us to death!"

"That's what I was thinking." Bill lay still for a while. "I want to go back, Harold, but I'm kind of afraid."

"Me too," said Harold. "But if we get the chance, I think as long as we do *exactly* as Promise-Keeper says, it'll be all right." He paused for a moment. "I hope we don't have to wait too long."

6

Before and Behind

Bill stood on the dock in his red swim trunks and wished he had never been born. He still wore his black and white shirt, although he had removed his running shoes and thrown his towel down on the beach. As long as he kept the shirt on he could put off the awful moment when he would have to either do a shallow dive or go back to the cottage and know he was the only one of the group who couldn't.

Harold was paddling around happily in the shallow water, looking for stones—nobody expected *him* to dive. Arthur Phillips, who had invited Bill and Harold down to his cottage at the lake, was already in swimming with the others. Arthur, his fourteen-year-old cousin Steve, the other cousin called Millie, who was Bill's age, and even the neighbor kid Shirley Ruth, who was only seven, had all run out along the dock, and one after the other, done shallow dives off the end.

Since Bill had never dived in his life, he had intended to wade in; but they had all tried to persuade him to jump.

"Hey, Bill, dive in off the dock! It's not over your head." This was Steve, the best swimmer in the gang and very careful.

Bill shook his head. "I don't know how," he called back. "I'll just walk in."

He didn't tell them that the thought of going head-first into that greenish water terrified him. When he was four he had fallen off a high dock into ten feet of water, and the memory of it was still with him. His dad had got him out, but not before he'd nearly drowned. He had never been able to forget the feeling of going down under the water, and although he'd learned to swim in Big McClintock, he had never wanted to dive, not even from a low dock like Arthur's.

"Aw, come on and try! There's nothing to it."

"Yeah—come on, Bill!" This was Millie, who was floating on her back and blowing water out of her mouth like a whale.

"Look, Bill—it's easy! Watch me!" Shirley Ruth, the seven-year-old, came in to where he was standing on the sand beside his towel and running shoes.

"Look!" she called, running back out along the dock to dive smoothly and disappear under the greenish water. A few seconds later she bobbed up, her short black hair wet around her face.

Then Bill walked out to the end of the dock. What else could he do after that?

Five minutes later, he was still standing there with his shirt on, miserably afraid, while they kept calling to him. He stared down at the water, greenish and solid looking and no more than two feet below the dock edge. In the shallow part you could see your feet, but not here. Bill felt that if he let himself go headfirst down into that lake he would never come up. The

65

water was an enemy, a green monster that was deep and thick, ready to smother him.

He *couldn't* let himself fall forward. Jump feet first, maybe, but head first—never, never!

"Just roll in. Bend your body over and just *roll* in," Arthur instructed.

"Don't think about it, *do* it," Millie advised.

Bill took off his shirt, slowly, unhappily, wishing he were home in Pillsbury. He hung it on the post beside him where it flapped in the breeze. He shivered a little and looked out across the lake, then up at the gulls wheeling lazily about. He wished he were a gull. He wished the UFO would come back and take him away forever. He looked up hopefully at the blue sky. Suppose a silver sphere appeared—?

There was nothing.

At last he looked down at the horrible greenish water. He bent forward, ready to roll in as Arthur had said to do. He put his hands together and took a deep breath. Now.

It was no good. He couldn't do it.

"Chicken!" called Millie. "Chicken! Chicken!" Bill stood there, curled over, ashamed to stand up but afraid to dive in, while the awful insult rang in his ears.

If only the UFO would come and take me away, he thought again, his face turning crimson.

And then, without warning, there was a sudden terrible barking behind him. He jerked his head around, not even straightening up his body, and saw, leaping out from the bush at the edge of the sand, a large black and tan police dog with a leash dangling from his collar.

"Prince! Prince! Come back! Come *back*!"A man was

66

running after him, shouting. The dog ignored him, and as his front paws hit the wooden planks of the dock, Bill realized those great white teeth were meant for *him*. He felt a fear, then, such as he had never known in his life.

He turned his head away and looked down at the water before him. It was no longer a monster but a friendly hiding place, a deep green blanket to cover him. It was like a thick quilt that could protect him from the awful white teeth.

He shut his eyes, took a deep breath, and rolled forward. The green water seemed to clutch his body and pull him down. He didn't care. The white teeth wouldn't get him. He felt his fingertips touch the sand, so he turned his hands up, kicked a little, and began to come back up to the surface.

He had done it! He had done a shallow dive!

For a second he forgot the dog; forgot even to see if it had followed him in. When the first bark reached his ears he remembered; and blinking water out of his eyes, he stood up and turned around to look at the dock a few yards away. The dog was still barking, but not at him. He was snapping and snarling at the checked shirt that flapped on the post!

The man, who by now had a firm hold on the leash, called out, "I'm terribly sorry. It's your shirt. He can't stand a checked shirt. Are you all right?"

"I'm OK," replied Bill, his eye on the leash. "But why doesn't he like my shirt?"

The man, a cottage owner named Kendall who, Arthur later informed them, had just moved in, began to explain. "Earlier this summer I had to put him in a kennel for two weeks. I found out later, from a kennel boy who quit, that Prince was badly treated by the owner. This man wore a checked shirt most of the time. Now Prince goes crazy every time he sees checks. I'm terribly sorry he scared you."

"That's OK," said Bill. "I don't hold it against him. If you'll tell me where your cottage is, I'll bring him a bone."

"You'll do *what*?" Mr. Kendall's mouth fell open.

"I'll explain when I come," muttered Bill while the gang laughed and hooted.

Later that day Bill, wearing a plain blue shirt, arrived at Mr. Kendall's cottage with the biggest bone Arthur's mother could find and told his story.

"You see," he finished, "I was afraid to dive, but what was behind me was worse!"

Mr. Kendall stared at him a few seconds and then he began to smile. "Bill," he said, "you remind me of a man named John Bunyan who knew all about fear before and behind—and wrote a book about it. I'll show you."

While Bill sat at the kitchen table drinking lemonade and watching Prince enjoy the bone, Mr. Kendall, after a few moments' searching in a large red-covered book called *Pilgrim's Progress*, began to read: "*If I go back to mine own country, that is prepared for fire and brimstone, and I shall certainly perish there; if I can go to the Celestial City, I am sure to be in safety there: I must venture. To go back is nothing but death: to go forward is fear of death and life everlasting beyond it: I will yet go forward.*"

"Why was he afraid to go forward?" asked Bill.

"He had to pass by two lions," said Mr. Kendall, shutting the book.

"Did he ever get to that place—that Celestial City?"

Mr. Kendall nodded.

"That sounds like pretty involved reading," Bill mused. "Maybe sometime I'll borrow it, if I may."

"I've got a better idea," said Mr. Kendall.

A week later a parcel was delivered to the beach post office from a city bookstore. It was addressed to Bill, and as he tore off the brown paper he wondered who would send him a present and why. Inside was a short version of *Pilgrim's Progress*, and written on the flyleaf were these words: *To Bill Baker, to mark the day he did his first shallow dive (with my help).* It was signed "Prince," and under the name was a black-pawprint.

Bill grinned and turned to the first page. He was glad that the UFO hadn't rescued him because now he had done the dive. He began to read the book, sitting in the sunshine on the bench outside the post office. He forgot about Promise-Keeper and became absorbed in the story.

For the time being he had no problems—but at that very moment, back in Pillsbury, the McGonigle family was moving into the house across the street.

7

Lily McGonigle

Bill lay on his back on the living room rug playing with Buster, the new pup that had arrived two weeks before, on his thirteenth birthday. He picked up the fluffy bundle of black fur, sat it on his chest, and looked into the small, impudent face.

"Buster," he said, "when you grow up I sure hope you never get stuck with a girl-dog like Lily Mc-Gonigle. Boy, I sure hope you don't!"

Harold, who had a half share in Bill's present, was standing at the window watching the first golden elm leaves drift down from the tree. "What's wrong with her?" he asked, turning around.

Bill put Buster back on the rug and gazed up at the ceiling. "She's always *there*, that's what's wrong! Everywhere I go, there she is! It drives me crazy!"

Harold looked puzzled. "Why don't you like her being around? Does she hit you?"

Bill sighed. Harold, at nine, obviously did not understand. "Hit me! I wish she would. No, she just always turns up behind me at school plays, or in front

70

of me in line—everywhere I go she gets there first and stands and smiles at me!"

"Don't you like her to smile?"

Bill shook his head. *"No.* She's ugly, and the boys tease me. 'Bill has a girl! Bill has a girl!' *What a girl!* Boy, how I suffer. It was a bad day for me when the McGonigles moved in across the street."

Harold turned back to the window. "Well," he said after a moment, "she's just come out of her house and she's looking this way—yep, she's coming over here. Should I go to the door?"

"No, it won't help. She'll just hang around until I come." Bill got to his feet and looked out. Lily McGonigle, in a faded blue sweatshirt and jeans, was coming up the walk and going around to the back.

In a few seconds the doorbell rang. It was Saturday noon, the third Saturday in September, and Mom and Dad had gone grocery shopping. At least that spared him hearing from Mom for the umpteenth time that he wasn't very nice to the new girl. Nice! He wished she'd drop down a hole and never come up. (Could only three weeks have passed since he'd come home from Arthur's to find she had arrived on the street?) He went to the back door.

"Yes?" he said, in what he hoped was a discouraging voice.

"Can Buster come out to play?" Lily smiled up at him through the screen. Her brown hair was pulled back and tied with a bow, and she looked a little neater than usual, but as his teacher always said about his writing, there was still plenty of room for improvement.

"I guess he can." He opened the door and let Buster

out. "But don't take him out of the yard—and be sure to shut the side gate when you go."

Lily was not easily discouraged. "I'm going to Sharon Allan's party this afternoon. She has a huge house on McClintock Road, and they're getting a magician, and I have a lovely new dress. It's blue nylon with pink velvet bows all down the front. You should see it."

Bill groaned inwardly. He hoped none of the boys playing down the block had seen her cross the street. Things were getting worse. Now she was coming into his yard! He would mention that she came to see the pup. He would say she was nuts about pups. It was true. She had picked Buster up and was cuddling him.

"Bill, can I be in your Morse Code Club? I've been learning it."

This was too much! "No!" He almost spat out the word. "The Nicodemus Club is for boys only. You can *never* be in it!" He felt satisfied to see the smile leave her face.

The phone rang.

"I gotta answer the phone, Lily. Don't forget to shut the gate." He looked at his watch. "It's twelve-thirty. Don't you have to go home and get ready for the party?"

He left her with Buster and escaped. The call was from Arthur Phillips. If they talked long enough she would probably go.

He was lucky. In a few minutes he heard the side gate click. Lily had given up. He settled down to the phone to make plans with Arthur for the next club meeting. He was glad Arthur couldn't see who had been at his back door.

At ten past one he hung up and went outside to see what Buster was doing. He had been quiet for some time.

The pup had disappeared!

Bill searched the yard, looking behind the garage and even under the big rhubarb leaves in the corner of the garden. There was nothing there but a rawhide bone. Finally he yelled to Harold, who was still in the house.

"Harold! Buster's gone! Go to McGonigles' and see if Lily remembers locking him in. That was half an hour ago! I'll run down to the highway—maybe she forgot." There was no time to lose. Jimmy Benson's pup had been killed on that highway, and Buster was only eight weeks old and pretty dumb about cars.

At twenty-five to two he was back in the yard. None of his friends who lived on the highway had seen Buster. It was then that he noticed the back gate. It had only appeared to be locked—the catch wasn't down all the way! A curious pup could easily have pushed it open and gone down the lane. Buster was clumsy, but he could run fast when he liked. By now he might be on Willowdale or even McClintock Road, which ran beside Big McClintock River. And that was no place for an eight-week-old pup.

Bill called to Harold, who was still searching behind McGonigles', and then began to run as hard as he could down the leaf-strewn lane toward Willowdale. Harold said Lily remembered locking the side gate. He wished he had noticed the back lock sooner.

He was opposite McClintock Park when he heard faint yelps coming from somewhere near the river. Ignoring the gravel paths, he raced across the smooth lawn to the low railing that marked the drop to the river's edge. From there he could see along the river path in both directions.

Far to the east, out on the end of a big sewer pipe, was a small black object, barking and looking down into the water.

Buster!

He whistled, hoping the dog would come. Buster turned sharply at the sound and then, to Bill's horror, lost his balance on the slippery metal and disappeared over the edge!

Bill jumped the low fence and began to run down the bank to the path. He could see Buster in the water, and now he was really scared. He knew that spot near the sewer pipe. A log thrown in there was soon drawn out to the middle, and he doubted the pup could fight such a current. Already he could see the small form moving away from the pipe, not toward it.

"Don't let him drown! Please don't let him drown!" he whispered under his breath. And then, because he was watching Buster, he didn't see the root sticking out of the rough, sloping bank, and his foot caught, throwing him full length on the ground.

As he raised his head from the dust a small blue figure emerged from the bushes where the path disappeared from view to follow the curve of the river.

Lily McGonigle!

In a matter of seconds she was out on the end of the pipe calling to Buster. Bill saw her glance back over her shoulder at him as he scrambled to his feet. Then Lily McGonigle, in her new blue party dress, jumped into the dirty waters of Big McClintock and began to wade out to Buster.

He watched her, waist deep, reach out until at last

her right hand grasped the small, black creature behind the neck. Then she lifted him up, wet and struggling and very much alive!

Buster was safe.

When Bill got to the pipe Lily was back up on the bank, the pup cuddled against her soaking, muddy dress.

"Lily! You got him! Boy, am I glad you were there!"

Lily, the ends of her hair wet and stringy, her dress a dripping ruin, smiled up at him.

"I'm glad too. I was supposed to meet Betty here so we could go to the party together. I came early so I could look along the river path for Buster. I'm glad I got him."

Bill remembered something. "You're pretty new here. Did you know about the current at the end of the pipe?"

"I guess I didn't." She looked down at the place where she had jumped in. "But I thought your pup was drowning." She smiled up at him. "It wasn't over my head, and anyway, I knew you were coming."

Bill was aware of boys' voices above them in the park. The kids must have come with Harold.

"Come on," he said. "We better go explain to your mother. You can't go to any party like that."

He walked up the path with Lily trailing behind carrying Buster, and he knew that, teased or not, he would walk her home.

He looked back at her and heard himself promising in a sudden rush of gratitude, "I'll try and get you in as a member of the Nicodemus Club."

As things turned out, he was to regret those words.

8

Wieners and Genes

It was Tuesday, October 13. Nearly a month had passed since Buster's rescue, and Promise-Keeper had still not returned. But at the moment Bill was thinking neither of Lily nor of the strange, golden figure. He was listening to Harold, who was complaining.

"Boy, oh boy!" his young brother moaned. "Why am I such a shrimp? How come I got born into a family of dwarfs! They let us try basketball this morning, and I might as well have been sitting down for all the hope I had."

Bill shrugged his shoulders. "Harold," he said, "you can't quarrel with your genes."

Harold looked down at his gray corduroys. "Jeans?" he sputtered. "How can I quarrel with my jeans? I'm not even wearing any! What kind of a dumb answer is that?" He glared at his brother.

Bill looked at his mother, who was making sandwiches, and they smiled at one another. "Listen, Harold," he said patiently, like Mr. Link, his new eighth grade science teacher, "genes are things on your chromosomes that you can't even see, but they decide how tall you'll be. You just can't quarrel with them."

"Things I can't even *see*, and they decide how *tall* I'll be? And what are chromo—chromothings? Where'd I get those?"

Bill sighed. "Harold, I can't give you a whole science course in my noon hour—you'll learn all about them when you get older."

Their mother spoke up. "Stop fussing. Being anxious won't add one inch to your height."

"Mr. Link says that scientists can make rats bigger with an extract from the pituitary gland," said Bill.

"How about getting me some of that?" asked Harold, his voice hopeful.

"He says it doesn't work too well with people." Bill began to grin. "However, in *your* case—"

Harold gave him a poke. "You're no giant."

"I know. But Mr. Link says boys do most of their growing between thirteen and fifteen, so there's still hope for us."

Mrs. Baker looked up from her sandwich cutting. "Listen, boys, what's in your head is more important than how much trouble you have walking under a low bridge."

Bill sat down at the table and began to eat his soup. In spite of his joking he felt depressed. He wished the subject hadn't come up. It reminded him of something he had been trying to forget: the program rehearsal after school, and the marching he had to do with Lily McGonigle as partner. Since she had saved Buster's life he didn't mind her being around—if only she weren't taller than him. If only *all* the girls weren't taller! It was agony looking up all the time!

And Miss Fowler, who taught English and was also his homeroom teacher, wanted everyone out for the program. Well, Friday it would be over, and then they were all invited to her place for a wiener roast after school. She lived outside of town, and some would go in her car and the rest by bus. That would be fun anyway. He cheered up a little.

His mother's voice cut into his thoughts. "Bill, I forgot to tell you. The sixth volume of your *Nature Encyclopedia* came this morning."

"Great!" He hurried through his lunch and spent the rest of his noon hour curled up in the big chair, lost in the wonders of volume 6. He forgot about the program, his size, everything.

The rehearsal was worse than he had expected. The principal came in and asked for ten boys to help move scenery. Bill was left with three other boys, also small for their ages but still taller than he was.

Miss Fowler spoke up. "While we're waiting for them to come back we'll do some extra marching."

The four girls came forward and took their places. Bill looked at Lily McGonigle, who smiled at him. *Down* at him.

His misery was complete. He wished Miss Fowler would go soak her head. Even her wiener roast wouldn't make up for this day.

He was out in the schoolyard, still thinking about how silly he felt marching beside Lily, when he discovered he had forgotten his math book. He walked slowly back through the empty halls to his room. Miss Fowler looked up from the table where she was sorting papers.

"Forget something, Bill?"

"My math homework."

"You're a responsible sort of person, aren't you?"

Bill stared up at her from his half-crouching position, one hand still reaching into his desk. She was smiling at him.

"Me?" He was stunned. What had he done right?

Miss Fowler nodded. "Yes, you. I know you don't like being in the program and marching with Lily and the other girls because they're taller than you. But you never try to goof off. You do your duty, Bill, and that's being responsible. You're very tall inside, Bill Baker."

On the way home he thought about what she had said. About being tall *inside*. It helped a little, it was something. But it would be better to be tall like Lily. Even as tall as Linda Tait, the class president. She giggled a lot and came late four days out of five, but she was the tallest person in the room.

On Friday the program was a success, and after it was over Miss Fowler began to tell them how to get to her place from the bus stop. Lily put up her hand.

"I can't come. My mom is on the four-to-midnight shift, and I have to mind Archie."

Miss Fowler frowned. "How old is he?"

"Two and a half." Lily's face brightened a little.

"Bring him along. You can look after him at my place as well as at home."

"Oh, thank you very much." Lily's smile was wonderful to see. "He's no trouble—he loves to eat. He eats everything in sight!"

Miss Fowler smiled. "That's all right. I have lots of wieners."

The thought crossed Bill's mind that now there

79

would be one smaller than him at the party. Hurray for Archie! Lily was a good egg. He was glad she could come.

They were on their second wieners when Lily discovered Archie was missing.

"Miss Fowler," she said, "I don't see Archie. Did he go in your house?"

Miss Fowler, now in jeans and a blue shirt, was just crossing the yard to the back door when a small figure in a red sweater emerged from a bushy area down at the end of the garden.

"There he is. Archie, come on back!"

The little boy approached, all smiles. There was mustard on his face, and he was carrying a flower. It was large and weedy looking, with big triangular leaves about eight inches long. The flower itself looked like a pale mauve morning-glory, but it wasn't.

Archie held up a green prickly seed capsule. "Pretty," he said. Then he went on chewing.

Bill looked at the plant and then more closely at Archie. He was horrified by what he saw. There was a bit of green leaf on the boy's lower lip. "Archie," he yelled, "open your mouth!"

Archie stared at him and then opened his mouth obediently, revealing a wad of half-chewed green material.

"Spit it out!" Bill shot his finger into Archie's mouth and began to pull out the unsavory mess. "Spit it out, Archie!"

"Oh, Bill, don't worry so much." Lily shook her head and turned back to the fire. "He'll spit it out."

"He better!" cried Bill. "That's Jimson weed! The leaves are poison. He could be awful sick." He looked at Miss Fowler. "He should go to the doctor right away."

Miss Fowler grabbed the plant from Archie and examined it. She turned to Bill. "How do you know it's poison? Are you sure?"

Bill nodded. "Absolutely. There's a picture of it in my *Nature Encyclopedia*, and it says grazing animals and children have been poisoned by eating it."

Miss Fowler looked at Archie. "All right," she said, "we can't take a chance. He may have swallowed a lot already." She turned to the class. "I have to drive Archie to the hospital. Lily, you come. The rest stay here." She looked at them all, her expression serious. "If any of you do anything crazy, or get hurt, I'll be in serious trouble for leaving you, but I can't take a chance with Archie. So I have to go."

She looked around the group again. Her gaze rested for a moment on Linda Tait and then passed on. She stopped finally at Bill. She seemed to be trying to decide something. At last she spoke. "Bill," she said, "I'm leaving you in charge. I think I can count on you." She turned to the others. "Remember, what he says goes."

She motioned to Lily. "Come on—let's get on our way." She scooped up Archie, and in a few minutes they were in her blue car bumping their way along the rutted mud road to the highway. The children stood watching. Finally they turned back to the fire and their forgotten wieners.

Leonard spoke first. "Lucky for Archie you know about plants."

Bill shrugged, reached for a bun. "I guess so. I hope he's OK."

81

Later that night he told his family what had happened. "The doctor said it was a good thing Miss Fowler brought him in right away. They found more of it in his stomach. But he's OK now. They pumped him."

"Did you have any trouble with the class?" his father asked.

"No. They knew it was serious. They like Miss Fowler."

Bill looked at Harold. "You know something, Harold? She left *me* in charge. Me, the shrimp! Not Linda. So cheer up. If you can't be tall, remember your math homework!" He grinned suddenly.

"Remember my math homework!" Harold stared at him. "How will that help me in basketball? Will it stretch my arms and legs?"

"No. But you won't mind so much. You'll feel tall inside."

Harold shook his head. "With ideas like that, I hope you never get on my team!"

Bill smiled. When it happened to Harold, he would understand.

Later, when Bill and Harold were in the family room, Lily turned up at the back door to ask if Buster was coming out. Bill called the dog and went with him into the yard to watch while Lily tried to teach him to fetch a little red ball she had brought. But after a few minutes she stopped, and ignoring the pup who waited expectantly at her feet, turned to Bill.

She looked down at the grass, then at a spot somewhere behind Bill's left ear. "I didn't come for Buster, not really. I really came to say thank you for what you did for Archie." She took a deep breath. "Look," she added, "about the Morse Code Club—I'm still practicing, and I want to get in more than anything in the world—" She paused a moment, her expression brightening momentarily. Then she went on, as though every word was being dragged out of her. "What I'm trying to say is that you're not—well, obligated. I mean that after Archie—" She stopped, looking at him helplessly.

This was a new side of Lily McGonigle. She was letting him off the hook. Bill looked at her closely and heard himself saying, "I promised you I'd try and get you in. I'll keep my word, if I can. Archie—well, what I did for Archie didn't cost me anything. Anyone could have done it. It's OK, Lily. I'll get you in."

"Bill!" She looked at him with such an expression of joy that he was glad he had said it, even though the words had hardly been out of his mouth before he'd regretted them.

"It's OK," he said hastily, moving toward the door. "I gotta go now, Lily. Put Buster in the house when you leave." He vanished inside, wondering if he was losing his senses.

She had opened the trap for him, and he had not escaped.

9

The White Shields of Abilan

The remainder of October passed; Halloween was celebrated by a party at Arthur's. Life jogged on, without excitement. Then came Saturday, November 28. The first snow of the year had fallen; the sky was gray, and the north wind promised frostbite for the careless.

"Four months and not a sign of Promise-Keeper," said Harold, looking out the kitchen window at Buster, who was snuffing about in the strange cold white stuff that had come down from the sky and hidden all his bones. "I sure wish we could get back in that garden. Imagine them having my marigolds, just like I planted them before Alfie dug them up!"

Bill smiled. "That was pretty neat. What I want to see again," he confessed, "is the Valley of the UFOs. If we could get back there, maybe Promise-Keeper— the real one—would give us a saucer. Then we could visit whenever we liked. Wouldn't that be great?"

Harold's eyes shone. "Boy," he exclaimed, "that would really be OK!"

Bill looked out at Buster, now four months old but still quite small. He was submerged in a drift. The sight of his black head sticking out of the snow reminded Bill of that awful day in September when Lily had pulled the pup from the river. What a mess it had made of her dress. And she had never complained. She had eventually gone to the party in some green thing she called her "school and second-best," whatever that meant. He remembered seeing her set off up the street, late.

He turned to Harold, distracted momentarily from the problem of how to get back to the land of the Small Ones.

"Harold," he said, his voice firm, "when the club meets tonight, I'm going to try again to get Lily accepted as a member. I have to do *something* about her. She mentioned it again yesterday, because she knows we meet tonight." He looked back at the pup, now running in wild circles around the yard. "I guess I should never have promised to try and get her in."

"Well, let her join. Why should anyone care? She won't cause trouble."

Bill shook his head. "I guess it's hard for you to understand how the gang feels about girls. They want the Nicodemus Club for boys only. But joining it is still the only thing Lily thinks about. She says she's been practicing the code every single night since September when she first heard about it from Arthur's cousin Millie. The one who was at the lake."

"Tell them they *have* to let her in. You're the president."

"You can't do that in a a a democracy," Bill protested. "She has to be voted in." He sighed, feeling the weight of Lily's great favor to him and his own sense of helplessness. Last month when he had suggested she be allowed to join, they had talked him down. "I'll just have to try again," he said. "You be around for the business part and do what you can, Harold."

"Sure," his brother agreed, plainly surprised that his influence should be considered worth having. He was a member himself only because he and Bill had formed the club and because it had started meeting at their house and did again now that the weather had turned cold.

Bill noticed Harold's expression and realized that in truth he must be desperate to settle the issue when he was counting on the gang listening to his kid brother! He took his parka from the hook behind the door. He knew he'd better get out and shovel a path before his parents arrived home from their grocery shopping.

That night, after he had called the meeting to order, he broached the subject of letting Lily join.

"I thought we settled that last month," said Pat. "Can't you keep her happy some other way?"

Bill shook his head. "I wish I could. This is the one thing she wants—to be in the Nicodemus Club. Don't ask me why."

Kelly laughed. "There's no need. She likes you!"

Bill groaned. "That doesn't help me. What am I going to say? She saved Buster's life. Don't you understand?" At that moment he would have given anything to be free of his rash promise to Lily.

"Well," began Arthur, "I think—"

"Look!" cried Harold, pointing to the floor beside Jim. "There's the UFO!"

He was right.

The same tiny silver disc that had first appeared on the family room floor last March was back. As they watched, it grew larger and larger, just as before, until at last it filled the end of the room. They moved out of the way, this time without fear. The door on the top popped open, and Promise-Keeper leaped out. He smiled at them all.

"I'm here to make you an offer," he said at once. "Let Lily join the club, and I'll take all of you with me tonight to my world."

"Say—how about that!" cried Pat. "I'd forgotten you! Now I remember, all of a sudden! We were by the clubhouse, and the black things came out of the trees and hurled arrows at us. . ."

Other voices joined in, exclaiming and interrupting one another.

"Yes, that's right! There was a storm—"

"The Dark Ones!" cried Bill, horrified, remembering.

He stared at the golden creature, who smiled at him. Then he turned and raced upstairs to his bedroom and grabbed the white stone from its hiding place in his desk. When he got back to the family room the rest of the boys were gathered around the UFO, which sat gleaming and sparkling on the blue tiles.

"Hold it!" Bill lifted his right hand and gently tossed the stone across the room. It hit the small, golden man on the chest and then dropped to the floor at his feet.

Bill and Harold, the only ones who knew why he had thrown it, watched and waited, their eyes fixed on the spot where the stone had touched the cloth.

Would the dark stain appear?

There was nothing. The gold shone and sparkled as before.

Kelly looked at Bill in astonishment. "Why'd you hit him? Are you *crazy!* He's going to take us to his world—in the UFO!"

Before Bill could answer Promise-Keeper laughed, and again they heard the sound of bells. He bent down and picked up the white stone and gave it back to Bill.

"Here," he said. "Guard it. You did right, Bill. You learned your lesson well." He turned to the others. "I'll explain to the rest of you later."

Bill tried to think clearly. He held up his hand. "What about the motion to allow Lily to join the club?"

"OK by me!" exclaimed Kelly.

"Whatever he says," added Greg, looking at Promise-Keeper. "As long as he takes us in the UFO."

Bill grinned at the small figure, who returned his smile, his silver-blue eyes flashing and twinkling. "Agreed?" he asked, looking at each boy in turn.

"Agreed!" they answered.

"Now," said Promise-Keeper, "if you will all line up and shut your eyes we'll begin the reducing."

"Harold doesn't have far to go," whispered Pat.

"Not up and down I don't."

"No talking, please. And whatever you do, keep your eyes closed until I give the word."

Bill felt as though he were in an elevator, going down at a tremendous speed. He wondered if the others felt it too, but he remained silent, as instructed.

He became aware that the floor and his feet were no longer in contact. He was floating.

What was Promise-Keeper doing? It took tremendous self-control not to peek.

"Only a minute more." The voice came from some-where above him. "Now you may all open your eyes."

They discovered that they were standing in a circle inside the UFO—at least Bill presumed they were in-side the UFO, since their surroundings were exactly as they had been in July when he and Harold had made their first trip. And they were the same height as Promise-Keeper, who was in the center of the group, smiling at them.

"You behaved very well. See how far we have come already." He motioned to the window beneath his feet.

They could see the great sphere that was their own planet rapidly receding from sight.

Finally Arthur broke the silence. "When will we get back?" he asked. "My mother's an awful worrier. If I'm late she won't let me come again. To the club, I mean!" he added, as the boys shrieked with laughter.

Promise-Keeper chuckled. "I promise you your mother will have no cause for anxiety," he soothed. "She will never even know you have been away. There is no earth time here. When you return, it will still be eight o'clock, and you will simply carry on with your meeting."

He looked down through the window and then stood quietly. "I will tell you about the Dark Ones and the white stones," he said, "and when I am finished, we will be there."

They listened while he explained why Bill had thrown the stone at him and then went on to describe the deceptive habits of the Dark Ones, who above all hated to see anyone discover the land of the Small Ones. "They would go to any length to wipe all memory of it from the minds of those who have entered. And that is the least of their evil," he added gravely, "so you must be extremely careful and do exactly as I tell you. It will be a long time before you can be trusted to get around safely on your own.

"Now," he concluded, "we are here, so I must ask you to once more shut your eyes until I give the word."

"Why do we have to do this?" asked Harold, obediently screwing his eyes tight shut.

"Yeah, why?" This was Kelly, who did nothing without a reason.

"You cannot know the 'why' of everything," said Promise-Keeper sternly. "If you wish to stay alive in this world, you must acquire the ability to obey *without* understanding if necessary."

"Who makes the rules?" asked Jim, keeping his eyes shut as directed.

"Rule-Maker," replied Promise-Keeper.

There was a slight jarring motion.

"Now," their host went on, "you may open your eyes." They were back in the incredible garden, bathed in golden light.

"Say—this is some place!" exclaimed Kelly. "May we look around?"

"Certainly," answered Promise-Keeper, "but stay with me inside the garden." He explained about the six-foot hedge.

Harold ran across grass as thick and soft as the deepest carpet and disappeared into a bushy area that bordered one side of the clearing. In a few moments they heard him call out, "Hey! Come and look at this! McClintock River! Big McClintock—and a fancy little house!"

The others began to run. Promise-Keeper followed at a walking pace, smiling at their excitement as he had when Greg had admired his leap through the air.

The bushes were thick, but they soon found the narrow path that Harold had followed. Bill arrived first. He looked where Harold was pointing and saw what at first sight certainly did seem to be McClintock Park and Big McClintock River, at the place where Buster nearly drowned. The same low railing edged the drop to the river path, but when he ran to look down at the water, he realized there was something missing. Quite a few things missing, in fact.

"Where's the sewer pipe," he called out, "and the old cans and rubbish? And all the mud? This isn't *our* McClintock—no way!"

The others, who had caught up with him, looked at the clean sparkling water edged with bright pebbles and tiny clumps of grass and flowers. As far as they could see, the river was bathed in soft light that frosted the ripples with flashing color; but when they looked up, they saw no sun. The light seemed to be everywhere and of equal intensity.

"Do you realize there are no shadows?" said Kelly, his voice awed. "This is really something—you better believe it!"

Harold spoke up, addressing Promise-Keeper directly. "Don't you have sewers?" he asked, crashing their thoughts back to earth.

"Maybe you don't eat?" supplied Bill, before Promise-Keeper could reply. "No food, no nitrogenous wastes—" He was showing off a bit, he knew, but there had to be an answer to this. If there was no food, that would account for the absence of sewer pipes, bottles, cartons, and other refuse.

Promise-Keeper smiled. "We have food, but not like yours. All of it is used, so we have no problem of waste disposal. Look behind you."

He was indicating the large clump of bushes through which they had just come. For the first time the boys noticed among the dark, glossy-green leaves some large white berries, each one about an inch in diameter.

Promise-Keeper picked a handful and gave them to Bill. "These are our White Berries. We eat nothing else."

"You mean you have these for *every meal?*" exclaimed Harold, horrified. "Don't you get awfully sick of them?"

Promise-Keeper smiled. "We would if they always tasted the same. But they don't."

"How can that be?" asked Bill. "On earth a white berry is a white berry." He selected one from his handful and turned it over and over between his fingers, feeling the firmness and smoothness of it.

"And it's a poison warning," chimed in Harold, thinking of something Bill had shown him in his Nature Encyclopedia. "Leaflets three, let it be; berries white, hide from sight," he recited.

Promise-Keeper shook his head. "Not here. The only poison we have is on the tips of the flaming darts the Dark Ones use."

"Where do they get it?" asked Bill, momentarily distracted from the idea of food.

"Yeah, where? It sure is powerful stuff!" added Kelly.

"There is a place they call the Black Cave. It comes from there. But to go back to our White Berries—Promise-Keeper looked at Bill. "What is your favorite dinner, Bill?"

Bill considered. "Roast turkey and dressing and all the Christmas stuff, I guess."

"Fine," said Promise-Keeper. "Now start putting the

berries into your mouth while you think of that dinner. Then begin to chew."

There was a moment of breathless silence while Bill's jaws worked. At last he swallowed and looked around at the boys. "He's right!" he cried. "The berries taste like turkey and stuffing and corn and—well, the whole bit!"

"Have you got any berries that taste like pepperoni pizza?" asked Harold, who had slightly missed the point.

"The berries are all the same," explained Promise-Keeper patiently. "*Your thoughts* make the change in them."

Moments later each boy had a handful, and the left bank of the restored Big McClintock began to resound with cries of joy and amazement.

"Chocolate sundae like I never tasted!"

"Double hamburger with onions!"

"Strawberry shortcake with real whipped cream!"

"Chicken and chips—with gravy!"

"Three-layer chocolate cake!"

Bill had stopped eating. "I'm full," he said. "I couldn't eat another crumb—I mean berry!"

"I should hope not!" said Promise-Keeper with a chuckle. "A handful the size you had is like Christmas dinner with seconds."

He turned to the rest of the group. "If you are now satisfied about how we eat, would you like to inspect the clubhouse?"

"The clubhouse!" cried Harold, suddenly remembering the little house he had seen.

Sure enough, on the riverbank at the far end of the clearing was a building which, in shape at least, resembled the clubhouse they had built south of Pillsbury, the shack where they had waited with Arthur for Promise-Keeper.

Harold reached it first. Moments later the others arrived, followed by Promise-Keeper at a more leisurely pace.

On close inspection, they saw that this clubhouse was built of plain gray stone. Instead of Inksters' discarded screen door at the entrance, it had only an arched opening cut into walls three feet thick. Set deep into the rock on the left side, a square window, empty of screen or glass, faced the clearing. The roof was flat.

"It's like a fort!" cried Harold, peering through the doorway. "Can we go in?"

"Certainly," said Promise-Keeper.

Inside, at first glance, they were aware only of the plain stone walls and floor and the rectangular wooden table with eight matching chairs. To their right, in the corner, was a large brown water cooler with brown mugs grouped at its base.

In the center of the table sat a red bowl filled to the brim with White Berries and beside it lay a large, thick, white book as big as the school dictionary.

Harold, being closest, was the first to notice the two-by-three-inch flat silver plates set into the table top, one in front of each chair. "What are these?" he asked.

Bill came over to examine them and discovered that the engravings on each plate were not, as he had expected, the names of the owners of the chairs, but the outlines of Morse code sending keys.

Promise-Keeper took from somewhere in his golden suit a silver rod shaped like a pencil. One end was pointed, the other round.

"Here, Bill," he said. "Measure a handspan above the plate and point the rod at it, round end down."

Bill obeyed while the others crowded around, watching intently.

What they had already seen happen to the UFO on the family room floor now began to happen to the engraving. It rose up out of the plate and took on thickness and shape, until in seconds a perfect silver replica of one of their own keys sat before them.

"Boy!" exclaimed Harold. "Did you see that?" He turned to Promise-Keeper. "Can I do one?" His eyes shone with excitement.

"You may all do one," replied the golden figure. "You must take turns, however, as there is only one rod."

They watched, fascinated, as Harold measured a span of his own chubby hand and then pointed the rod. In moments, a second silver key sat before them!

The rod passed to Arthur, Jim, Pat, Kelly, and finally Greg. When each boy had used it, Bill turned to Promise-Keeper. "I didn't know you used Morse code here," he said.

The others looked up, their attention caught.

"We don't. These keys have been designed for the people for whom the clubhouse was built. The eighth, of course, is in case Lily should attend a meeting here."

They noticed, suddenly, the empty chair and extra plate.

"You mean they were made for *us*?" cried Bill. "I thought—I thought they belonged to someone special—like royalty!" He was aware that the others were as amazed as he was.

"Are they real silver?" asked Jim.

"Our form of silver," replied Promise-Keeper. "They

are designed so that you may use the talent you have on earth when you are working here for our Department of Encouragement."

"Department of Encouragement! How can we work for that?"

"Who does it encourage?"

Promise-Keeper looked around the group, his eyes resting for a moment on each boy. He began to speak, his voice grave.

"Suppose, for example, the Dark Ones were attacking heavily in some special area on earth—or any other planet, for that matter. They do all the time, of course. If you were here, The Department of Encouragement would arrange for you to send messages into the minds of those under pressure. You would help them remember that we exist and that we are able to get rid of the Dark Ones. You could even encourage them to come here."

"Is the code understood everywhere?" asked Bill.

"Oh, no," replied Promise-Keeper. "You are allowed to use it because knowing it is your Earth talent—it will be automatically translated for the receivers into thoughts in their own language, whatever it is. This sending equipment is only enough like yours that you can operate it. Actually it is highly specialized, and for the present you will have to be content to use it without understanding how it works."

"That's OK," Bill agreed. "But where do we get the right messages?"

Promise-Keeper drew their attention to the large white book.

"In there," he replied, "you will find messages of encouragement suitable for every possible situation and planet, including your own. We hope you will work for us this way when you visit."

"Why sure!" Bill said. "We'd be glad to, wouldn't we?" He looked at the others.

"You better believe it!" Pat declared.

"Good," said Promise-Keeper. "Now, before I leave I want to show you how to enter the walls."

"Enter the walls!" cried Harold. "Are they hollow?"

Promise-Keeper nodded and walked over to the stone wall facing the doorway. For the first time they noticed that in its center was a silver disc the size of a quarter. Holding the silver rod in his outstretched hand, Promise-Keeper turned to Bill.

"Here," he said. "Stand three feet back and point the sharp end at that spot."

"Three exact feet?" asked Bill. "I don't have a ruler."

"I know." Promise-Keeper smiled. "I mean three of your feet."

Bill measured backward, toe to heel, three steps from the wall and pointed the rod. For a second nothing happened. Then, very slowly, the wall began to move to the right.

"An electric door!" said Kelly. He turned to Promise-Keeper. "What if the next guy to open it has really big feet? Would it work?" He glanced down at the place on the stone floor where Bill stood. "I don't see any mat like they use in stores—to cover the switch, I mean."

"We don't need one. This only looks like your electric door," explained Promise-Keeper. "Here the power is in the rod. Big feet, little feet—it doesn't matter. The correct distance is calculated in relation to the one who holds the rod." He smiled at the rest of the group. "Our method does have one factor in common with yours, however. No door, or wall, opens until the person is directly in front of it, ready to enter.

"Look!" cried Harold, who had not been paying much attention to how the wall opened.

The stone surface, for surface was all it was, had been gradually reduced, like the UFO, until it was a narrow strip at the extreme right corner. Now what was revealed commanded their full attention.

Set into the back wall of the cavity were four silver shelves, each bearing a heap of cloudlike, filmy material. The bottom two were only a few feet off the floor, but the two directly above must be reached by using a silver ladder that leaned against the rock between them.

"Those are your beds," said Promise-Keeper. "Please try them out. There are four more just like them." He took the silver rod from Bill and went to the right-hand wall.

"Is that ever neat!" murmured Greg a few moments later when it too was open.

"Try them," urged Promise-Keeper. "You will find the covers warm and very soft. They are better than any mattress or sleeping bag you have ever used."

Within seconds the first four boys to reach the walls were climbing up the ladders and the last three, of whom Harold was one, lay stretched out on the lower shelves.

Bill, who was directly above Harold in the right half of the end wall, found that Promise-Keeper had spoken the truth. He had never been so comfortable, and looking down at himself, was amazed to find the filmy substance opaque. To an onlooker only his head would be visible.

"Should you wish to sleep in the clubhouse, you must use these beds and shut the walls," said Promise-Keeper. "You will find there is good air circulation through concealed slits in the upper foot of rock."

"Why must we shut the walls?" asked Bill.

"Only inside the rock are you safe from the Dark Ones," replied Promise-Keeper.

"But why aren't we safe just being in the clubhouse?" asked Kelly, getting up on one elbow and looking down from his upper shelf in the side wall. "It's the same rock." He ran exploring fingers over the slightly rough surface over his head.

"Because out here you are not completely surrounded by it," answered Promise-Keeper. "There is a door and a window, which are necessary for you to have light and communication with your environment, but which leave you open to attack. Remember what I told you on Earth—once the Dark Ones have seen you, neither that clubhouse nor this can hide you. Your shields and white stones are your only defense. While you are sending messages, you must be alert and ready to protect yourselves. But when you want to sleep, go inside the rock. You will be completely hidden and quite safe—but only if you shut the walls."

"But how can we ever sleep here?" asked Arthur, suddenly sitting up on his bedshelf with a worried look. "Our parents would have the police looking all over Pillsbury for us!"

"Did you forget?" said Promise-Keeper. "Our time here is not the same as earth time. You can stay here as long as you like, and when you return to your planet it will be the same time as when you left."

"Then we can have all our meeting here—"

"Not just meetings!" interrupted Bill excitedly. "Just think—we could stay for *ages*! It could be like a holiday, or a camping trip."

"We could even come in the middle of the school year!" cried Kelly, who hated the long months of winter and staying indoors. "Then when we decided to go back, it would still be the same day, and we could start again where we left off!"

"We could take off right in the middle of class," exclaimed Bill. "And we'd never be missed!"

The boys all began talking at once about the great times they would have, a zillion miles from earth, all on their own, sending messages from their new clubhouse and exploring the incredible land of the Small Ones.

The small golden figure with the silvery eyes smiled as he listened to the happy voices. Finally he raised his hand to silence them.

"We will see," he said. "It is not yet certain how often you will be able to come. There are many dangers, and many secrets you must learn before you can be truly at home here. But we will see.

"For the present," he went on, stepping inside the end wall, "I will show you how to get out of your hidden dormitory after you have slept."

He turned to Harold, who was sitting in his bunk, and said, "On the rock at the foot of your bed is another silver disc. You will be responsible for opening and closing both walls. From the inside, they operate together. It can be done while you are lying down."

"Suppose I need a drink of water?" asked Harold. "They'd all get waked up."

"Get one before you come in here," said Promise-

Keeper with a smile. He handed him the rod. "Point the round end at the disc," he said.

"Will you stay there?" asked Harold. "Just in case—"

"Certainly. I understand."

"Just a minute," called Jim from his bed under Kelly. "How would we get out if he's asleep? We don't have a rod."

"Press the silver disc you will find on your side on the adjoining wall. Harold will be awakened by a buzzer."

"You better have sharp ears, Harold," said Jim. "No way do I want to get trapped in here!"

Harold looked at Promise-Keeper. "How loud is the buzzer?" he asked.

"Loud enough that you will always hear it," Promise-Keeper assured him. "You are the youngest, and for this purpose your hearing is the most acute. If you had not already chosen this place I would have assigned it to you."

Harold called out, his voice very loud, "Get ready, you guys! I'm closing the walls!"

He raised the rod and slowly both walls began to expand back into place, until the boys were in total darkness.

"Fine," came the voice of Promise-Keeper. "Now try opening them. Use the pointed end."

"How?" asked Harold. "I can't see the spot."

"Raise the rod and you will."

He was right. The moment Harold obeyed, a faint light came from the end of the rod, just enough to enable him to aim correctly. The walls began to shrink back again.

"Now," said Promise-Keeper, leaping lightly to the floor outside, "you may look around as much as you wish. Later on a Small One will come to show you how to use the book and operate the sending keys. But for now you may explore the garden if you like. Just be sure to close the walls if you leave the clubhouse. There is a disc on the window wall, at the corner. Use the round end of the rod, of course." He looked up at Bill. "When you are outside the walls, Bill must take care of the rod."

"Right," said Bill, starting to descend his ladder.

The others followed his example. Promise-Keeper had already gone outside. "I must go for your shields," he called. "Remember, on no account leave the garden."

"What kind of shields?" asked Jim.

"The white shields of Abilan. The arrows are unable to penetrate Abilan. It has other powers, but there is no time to explain that now."

"Is it like asbestos?" asked Harold, who found fire and all things connected with it extremely fascinating.

"You might say it was our version of your asbestos."

Promise-Keeper began to walk across the clearing. The boys watched from the door and window until he disappeared into the bushes.

For the next twenty minutes they stayed in the clubhouse, examining it in detail, shutting and opening the walls, and crowding around to get drinks from the cooler.

"It tastes like water from that mountain spring, the one in Fraser Canyon—remember, Bill?" asked Harold, refilling the brown mug on which he had discovered his name carefully lettered in white.

"I remember. When I swallow it I can almost hear the sound of the water splashing over the stones—"

"That's the rocks in your head," teased Jim, grinning at his own joke.

"I think I'll just have another chocolate sundae," said Arthur, dipping into the red bowl and taking out a few berries.

"Let's go outside before Arthur throws up!" Jim jeered

loudly, heading for the door. In a few minutes the others trooped out after him, Bill last, after carefully closing the walls.

He stood in the doorway a moment, looking at the table where the sending keys once more lay concealed in their plates. He still couldn't believe the clubhouse was theirs. When he turned around he discovered the boys had already begun to scatter in all directions among the shrubs and trees.

"Remember what Promise-Keeper said!" he called out. "Nobody leaves the garden without him. Nobody!"

He went around to the back of the clubhouse and started to follow one of the little paths into the forest. After a few minutes he began to wonder if he might be in the very same wood through which he and Harold had gone to reach the Valley of the UFOs.

Hurrying along, he rounded a large clump of White Berry bushes and came to a sudden halt. He was facing the six-foot hedge that marked the boundary of the garden.

Beyond this point they had been forbidden to go.

He looked along the hedge to the right and saw towering above it, on its other side, a huge and familiar-looking outcrop of gray rock, topped by a single scraggly little pine that leaned sideways as though about to tumble down to the unseen path below. This peculiar landmark, which he recognized at once, was all the proof he required to know that the path on which he walked must be very close to the path from Stump Lake. He need only go through the hedge, and he would be on his way to the Valley of the UFOs!

He could hear the voices of the others in the distance. It would take but a moment to slip through and just take a peek to make sure. He took a few steps and then stopped.

Surely the real Promise-Keeper would take them all to the valley when he returned with the shields. Suddenly the thought of deliberately disobeying this strange person, who seemed so busy doing wonderful things for all of them, was very distasteful.

He swung around and began to run back toward the others, afraid that his curiosity would get the better of him if he hesitated even a second longer. In a few minutes he was in sight of the clubhouse.

"Remember—stay in the garden!" he shouted to the other boys, who were still wandering about in the woods. The boundary hedge very likely cut across the other paths, and they would also be tempted to go through, if only to see what lay beyond.

"What could happen if we left it?" asked Greg, popping up from behind a White Berry bush.

"You could be attacked, like we were at the other clubhouse. Or a Dark One in disguise might lead you over the cliff, and you'd land back home. Like happened to Harold and me last time. Or worse," he added, taking his cue from Promise-Keeper. He wasn't exactly sure what he meant by "worse," but Promise-Keeper had said that the danger outside the garden was enormous.

"Yeah, last time!" Jim and Kelly came over. "Why didn't you tell us about that?"

"You wouldn't have believed me. After the attack at the clubhouse you didn't even remember *seeing* Promise-Keeper and the saucer. Only Harold could remember properly, and I was able to believe what he said because I could recall bits and pieces of what had happened. Perhaps I didn't get hit in as many places as you did. After the trip in July, it was all quite clear again because the Dark Ones didn't poison us."

"How come Promise-Keeper took you two anyway? What did you do to make him come for you?"

"I don't know," Bill said, shaking his head. "I just don't know, and he won't tell us. He says we have to learn the secret for ourselves. I guess we're just lucky."

"You sure are. I wish—"

His words were cut short by a sudden terrible shrieking above their heads. They looked up into the trees, as did the boys who were in the other parts of the garden, and they were horrified by what they saw: hundreds of small orange flames glowed among the green leaves.

The Dark Ones had returned.

The sound of their shrieking filled the whole garden. It had a nerve-shattering effect, and the boys began to run about, looking up, trying to find a tree that had no black creature crouching in its boughs waiting to swoop down.

There was no such refuge. Every tree was full of the disgusting black beings. Here and there a head could be seen clearly, and the sight of the awful black eyes, glistening like slimy pools, peering at them from between tangled strands of lifeless black hair, produced panic.

"Don't look at their eyes! Get in a group!" cried Bill wildly, trying to form the boys into a circle with Harold in the center.

They huddled together, glad to have a leader arise among them and give an order they could obey. Just as before, they stood with the right side of each boy overlapping the left side of his neighbor.

When this happened, there was a momentary lull in the screaming noise above their heads. For a moment it seemed as though their attackers might be about to leave, for each dark figure rose from its

105

crouching position and stood upright, arms extended above wildly streaming hair. But then, with another chilling scream, they swooped—not away, but down to the grass where they formed a large, deep circle around the boys.

Bill became aware that opposite him, in the inner ring, was a figure slightly taller than the rest, with longer hair and even more dreadful eyes. As this white-faced, vampirelike creature, evidently the leader, raised his right arm, Bill noticed that his hand was not made of the same grublike flesh as the rest of his body. The thumb, fingers, and palm were silver in color, and although their movement was fleshlike, their appearance was hard and cold like metal. Obviously this raised metallic hand was a signal for attack. Within seconds hundreds of silver, flame-tipped arrows were poised above the heads of the Dark Ones, enclosing the boys in a solid ring of fire.

"Our shields!" cried Bill. "Where are our shields?"

At that moment, as though his words had created them, seven white oval shields appeared above them, hovering in the air, each within grasping distance of a boy.

"Six around and one on top!" rang out the voice of Promise-Keeper from somewhere over their heads.

Bill grabbed the shield nearest him by its small, inner strap, and helped Harold center another directly over himself and the group. Kelly, Arthur, Greg, Jim, and Patrick filled in the circle with the remaining five. There was a fierce screaming from the Dark Ones, and the fiery arrows were hurled in upon the beehive formation of shields.

To the boys' amazement, they were unharmed. Just as Promise-Keeper had said, the fiery tips were unable to penetrate the thick, white, chalky Abilan and fell sputtering to the ground.

Unfortunately for Arthur, there was a space in front of him where the shields were imperfectly lapped. Curious to see his attackers, he peered out and was rewarded with a flaming arrow which struck him above the eye, causing him to jump back and nearly drop his shield.

"Careful!" cried Bill, who stood next to him. He had wondered why the Dark Ones bothered to attack when they knew the quality of the shields, but now he understood. There was always hope that those who held them would leave gaps or drop them under pressure.

"There must be hundreds of them!" exclaimed Arthur. "We haven't a hope! Any second they'll rush us! Can't we *do* something?"

"Hold steady," came the voice of Promise-Keeper.

Arthur rubbed the spot above his eye. "Bill," he whispered, "why not throw your white stone at them— remember before how they disintegrated when the stones hit them?"

"You may throw the stone." Again the voice of Promise-Keeper came to them from above.

Bill obeyed, hurling it awkwardly through a tiny gap between the top of his shield and Arthur's. It struck one of the creatures in the chest before dropping to the ground a short distance in front of the boys. The result was astonishing. Not only did the one hit begin to disintegrate, but those on each side of him backed away in horror, breaking their circle and dropping the fresh arrows they had been about to hurl.

"We've got to get that stone back!" cried Arthur, darting out and back before anyone realized what he was doing. "If only we had more," he wailed when he was once more safely behind his shield, "so we could finish them off. It's no good standing here waiting for them to rush us!"

It was then that Bill remembered the pile of white stones near the cliff edge. There must have been three dozen or more!

"Follow me!" he yelled, forgetting to wait for instructions from Promise-Keeper. "Everybody follow me!"

He broke the circle and, holding his shield above him as protection, began to run toward the path into the woods. He heard the sound of the other boys running along behind him and the shrieks of the black creatures who, seeing the shield formation broken, began to rain arrows into the group.

Running was a poor idea.

The big shields were heavy and awkward, perfectly designed for shelter in hive formation, but ill-formed to carry in flight. There was much stumbling and gasping, and the boys at the rear suffered many pricks from fiery arrow tips. Getting through the boundary hedge was awkward too, though they managed it. On the other side, as Bill had suspected, the path joined up with the one from Stump Lake.

"We're nearly there!" he yelled over his shoulder. "We're going to make it!"

They ran on, their speed hindered badly by the shields, until at last they became aware that the woods was thinning out. Within seconds the opening that led to the Valley of the UFOs was visible, and they took fresh courage.

Patrick's voice stopped their flight. "Look!" he called. "They're leaving!"

As their eyes followed his pointing finger, they realized he was right. For no apparent reason their pursuers had turned back and were streaking through the trees like ragged black birds, to vanish from sight at last in the blue patches of sky that peeped between the thick green foliage. The boys stood in a cluster staring after them, grateful for a chance to catch their breath.

"I wonder if they'll come back?" asked Arthur.

They became aware of the figure of Promise-Keeper standing before them on the path. "There's no need," he said, his expression sad. "Their work is done."

"But now we can go to the valley!" cried Bill. "It's right through there—you can see the opening in the trees!"

"Can you?" asked Promise-Keeper.

Bill looked again and realized to his horror that the woods were beginning to fade.

"Oh no!" he cried, seeing too late what had happened. He turned back to the golden figure. "But they would have rushed us. You said I could throw the stone!"

"*That* stone," replied Promise-Keeper. "If you had only remained in your position, you would have been rid of them all, without harm, and then we could have gone to the valley."

"Rid of them? How?" asked Kelly. "We weren't *doing* anything!"

"Yes, you were. If you had held your position, they would have begun to disintegrate from the effect of looking at your shields."

"Wouldn't they have rushed us?"

"No. They can tackle a single shield and sometimes take it from you, but the hive formation is fatal for them. Sooner or later, they would have left. They know

109

that to remain too long near a shield hive means eventual disintegration, the same as when they are hit by the white stones. The hive attack is slower but just as certain in the end if you have patience."

"We didn't know! Why didn't you tell us?" cried Arthur.

"You never gave me time. You took things into your own hands," replied Promise-Keeper sadly.

"*I* did," said Bill. "*I* spoiled it."

"Your mistakes are part of your training," said Promise-Keeper gently. "To learn to take orders and to trust your safety to someone else is the most difficult lesson of all."

Slowly he began to fade, along with the woods, the path, the sky.

"I'm sorry," cried Bill. "Can we come back?"

The voice of Promise-Keeper was very faint. "You can come when you—"

The voice was gone.

"The next item of business," said Bill, "is, What shall we do for our Christmas meeting?" He stopped suddenly, looked at Harold, then at the rest of the Code Club members sprawled around in the family room. "Why does everyone have black specks on their faces?" he asked, puzzled. "Do I?"

Harold looked at him. "Yes, you do."

Bill looked around the room again. They were all marked in the same way. He took out his handkerchief and rubbed his face, looking at the dark smudges on the white cloth. A clouded memory of a small, golden creature stirred, struggled, and slipped away again.

"I can't figure it out," he mused. He looked down at the notebook on the table, in which the minutes of the meeting were recorded. "Harold," he said, "I've forgotten something. As I am not allowed to make a motion, would you do it for me?"

"Oh yes," agreed Harold, also remembering. "I move that Lily be allowed to join the club."

"I second that," said Greg.

"Any discussion?"

There was none.

"All in favor?" Bill was puzzled. There was no opposition at all. Six hands were raised.

"Motion carried."

Later he spoke to Harold about it. "I don't get it," he said. "I just don't get it."

Before it all came clear, there would be something else he *would* get, something he didn't want at all—a dreadful scarf, knitted for him by that most troublesome of girls, Lily McGonigle.

10

True Citizens

It was a terrible scarf. As a knitter, Lily McGonigle was long on effort but short on talent. Bill held it out at arm's length, the whole five feet of it, in all its blue and yellow eye-smashing glory.

"It looks like some kind of flag," said Harold, "or a school banner." He picked up the end, holding it by the fringe, which was six inches long. "It's full of holes, too. It's a mess."

"You're not kidding. So what can I do with it?" Bill looked at his mother. "Surely you don't expect me to *wear* this thing?"

His mother frowned and shook her head. "I know, Bill. It's pretty awful. I don't think Lily has ever knitted anything before. It must have taken her hours and hours. Couldn't you wear it at least to her party tomorrow night? She'll be looking for it on you."

"Looking for it! How could she miss it! Wearing this will be like going out wrapped in a flag with built-in drums. Why, oh why, did Lily have to give me a Christmas present at all? I didn't expect one. I didn't want one!"

Bill threw the gift down on a chair. Buster grabbed the end of it and started tugging. Bill looked at him, so healthy and full of fun, and groaned.

"Will I never be done with Lily McGonigle?" he muttered. "Leave it alone, Buster. It's got enough holes without adding any." He rolled it up then and shoved it back in the fancy red and gold box Lily had wrapped with such care.

Christmas morning! A person was supposed to be happy on Christmas, not have his whole day ruined by an unwanted gift! He thought of the reaction of the gang if he arrived at the party tomorrow night in this evidence of Lily's devotion.

It was just like Lily to have a special party in honor of the Nicodemus Morse Code Club because they had finally made her a member. There were to be fourteen kids altogether, but the seven club members were the reason for the party. Her dad and her Uncle Harry were driving them all out to the big slide near the clubhouse, across the road from Humber's farm. Her mom was making a regular feast for when they came back—hamburgers, potato chips, hot chocolate, and then a huge chocolate cake for dessert.

Bill shook his head. Lily meant well, but she had just overdone it. Without the scarf, which she would naturally expect him to wear, he could have looked forward to a good time. He picked it up in its box and headed for the stairs. He would put it away in his room and try and forget all about it for the rest of the day.

With the help of his other presents and all the excitement and the turkey dinner, he managed quite well, but by seven o'clock the following evening the problem was back on his hands. At first he thought he would be able to brazen it out. He and Harold stood

113

on the front steps of McGonigles', ringing the bell and waiting for Lily to answer the door.

"Hi!" she said, smiling as she opened it. "You're the first here. I—" She stopped suddenly. "Bill, you aren't wearing the scarf—I guess it wasn't any good."

Bill looked at her, at the absolutely woeful expression that slowly replaced her smile. It spread from freckle to freckle across her face, till she was the saddest looking girl he had ever seen. His desperate plan to arrive at the party, pretend he had forgotten the scarf and then not take time to go back, began to fall apart under the impact of her great and obvious disappointment. He knew, then, what he had been trying not to know since the moment he first saw the gift. He would *have* to wear it, at least to her party. Her feelings were more important than his embarrassment.

"The scarf?" He looked down at the front of his gray parka, pretending surprise. "Well, whadda you know? I must have left it on the chair! I can't go without my new scarf, can I?" He turned on his heel, trying to smile. "Back in a minute!"

Harold stared at him, eyebrows raised, and there was a scrap of comfort in knowing that at least one person realized the enormous sacrifice he was about to make for Lily.

At home he ran upstairs to his room, grabbed the scarf, flung it around his neck and rushed out again, aware of his mother's astonished glance when he met her in the downstairs hall.

He arrived back at Lily's door, as ill luck would have it, at the same moment as Pat and Arthur.

"Wow!" said Arthur. "Get a load of that!" He picked up the bright blue and yellow end that dangled over

Bill's left shoulder. "It sure has a lot of holes. What happened to it?"

Pat spoke up. "That's where the stitches were dropped. My mom knits a lot, and when she was teaching my sister I heard her saying to be careful not to drop stitches, or there'd be holes."

"Whoever knit that should go in for strainers," said Arthur, smiling at his own joke.

"Knitted strainers!" Pat laughed, picturing them all soggy and wet, full of spaghetti. He began to describe them to Arthur.

"Shut up, you guys," Bill whispered fiercely. "*Lily* made it!" As he spoke, the door opened and Lily herself stood there.

When she saw the scarf her smile began to return, spreading and glowing like the rising sun. "Bill," she murmured, "you're wearing it!" She motioned them inside, obviously entranced by the visible evidence that her hours of work had not been wasted.

When Jim, Kelly, and Greg arrived, any comments they might have made were influenced by Bill's loud announcement: "How do you like my new scarf? Lily made it!" He had decided that if he *had* to suffer, he might as well spare Lily if he could. They stared at it, obviously impressed, but restrained themselves to "Pretty sharp," "Real neat," and "Great color." Bill was certain he would hear more later.

Soon Mrs. McGonigle was waving good-bye to them all from the front door. She had Archie by the hand, and looking at him, Bill remembered the Jimson weed. No matter what he did, his life seemed to get mixed up with Lily McGonigle's. He squeezed back into his corner of the car—Lily's dad's car, of course! Coming back, he would try to get in her Uncle Harry's.

Half an hour later, he stood on the top of the hill and watched Lily and her six girl friends shooting away down the icy slide on the eight-seater. It was a beautiful night for a toboggan party. A bright moon and no wind to freeze your face. Maybe he would have a good time after all.

"I didn't want to say anything before"—Kelly's voice broke into his thoughts—"because she's putting on the party, but isn't it time you did something about Lily?"

"What would you suggest?" asked Bill fiercely, realizing that Kelly had just been waiting for this chance. "Should I drown her?"

"The river's frozen," said Harold. "You better wait till spring."

"Why wait till spring? Do it *now*!" hollered Jim, who considered himself a wit.

"You didn't have to *wear* that thing," Arthur commented. "Really you didn't."

"I did," said Bill.

"What did she do? Threaten to choke you with it?"

"No!" snapped Bill. "She just looked at me. Like Buster does when you say he can't come with you."

He turned away, grabbed the rope of the toboggan, and flung himself down in the first seat, crossing his legs under the curved top. "Come on!" he said. "Let's move! We didn't come here to talk!"

Harold got on behind him, and the other five boys scrambled into the remaining places. There was a moment when they teetered on the edge, and then they were off.

Swooping through the air down the steep slope, over icy snow that sparkled with moonlit diamonds, Bill forgot all about the teasing and embarrassment the scarf had caused him. For the first time since Christmas morning he was completely happy. The cold air stung his cheeks, and he hunched down in his seat.

"Yahoo!" he yelled. "Here we go!"

They went much farther than the girls had, and they laughed in derision as they flew past the tumbled heap of arms and legs and heads that spread out from Lily's toboggan where it had come to a halt a little way out from the end of the slide.

It was just as their own pace began to decrease that Bill saw it—sitting on the ice near the bank on the far side of the river.

The UFO! Sparkling and gleaming at the edge of the bushes, it reflected the moonlight on its silver surface.

Harold saw it, too. "Look!" he yelled. "The UFO!"

And then Bill had the surprise of his life.

"A UFO?" exclaimed Kelly.

"Where?" asked Pat.

"I don't see any!" cried Arthur, looking up at the sky.

"Over there!" Bill pointed. "It's no more than a hundred feet away. Right *there!*"

It was no use. Of all the seven, only he and Harold could see it.

"It's the poison," said Harold. "I guess it hasn't worn off them."

They tumbled from the toboggan and began to run across the ice to the shining craft, leaving the other boys staring at them and looking vainly toward the bushes. They saw the door on the top pop up and Promise-Keeper jump out. Suddenly they realized that Lily had left the girls and was running, too.

Lily could see it!

They watched as Lily reached the UFO. Promise-Keeper smiled and spoke to the astonished girl as she stared open-mouthed, then he beckoned to Bill and Harold. "Come on," he urged. "We have to hurry."

"Where are we going?" asked Bill, gently touching the golden figure with the white stone which he had put in his parka pocket. It had gone everywhere with him since November 28, although he had had no clear memory of where it had come from or why he felt compelled to carry it around. No dark stain appeared.

"To my world," the golden figure replied, smiling at Bill. "Your shields are ready in the garden for you. Guarding them is an escort of Small Ones with enough white stones to get you safely to the valley. All that I had planned for you last time, and the time before, will take place tonight." He paused a moment. "Of course you must wait for the escort."

Bill nodded. "You bet we will. This time I won't get so smart!" The thought of what lay ahead swept over him in a huge wave of delight. How had it come about?

"Are we really to get our own UFOs?" asked Harold.

"Yes," answered Promise-Keeper. "One for each of you."

Through all of this Lily had stood, spellbound, gazing raptly from the spacecraft to Promise-Keeper to Bill and back. Now she looked again at Bill and spoke for the first time. "I'd much rather be in yours. I don't want to be alone in one of these—whatever they are!"

Bill sighed, then grinned. "Well, I guess if you really want to it's OK."

Promise-Keeper nodded. "For this time." He looked at Lily. "I realize you are a bit bewildered just now, but Bill and Harold will tell you all about it. You will have to handle your own eventually, you know."

118

She nodded too. "Yes," was all she said.

"Won't the gang wonder where we are when we get into your UFO? They can't see it," said Bill, suddenly remembering them all.

Harold laughed. "I bet they think we're talking to the bushes."

"Hardly." Promise-Keeper smiled. "Look at them."

They did, and at that moment they knew something tremendous had happened to them.

There, toiling up the hill with the two toboggans, were fourteen figures, seven boys and seven girls. And among them were *Bill and Harold Baker and Lily McGonigle.*

"But we are *here*!" cried Bill, staring. "How can we be *there*?" He turned to Promise-Keeper. "They aren't paying any attention to us. Don't they see us here? When—I mean how—"

"I agree it seems confusing," said Promise-Keeper with a sympathetic nod. "It's because you can't understand how two worlds can go on at the same time. The moment you spoke to me tonight you became part of my world in a way you have never been part of it before. However, your friends are not aware of this change in you, and they still see you with them at the party. Either they have never seen me, or they have seen me and forgotten me, through the work of the Dark Ones."

He paused a moment and looked across the river at the group that had reached the top of the slide. "Tonight, as soon as you spoke to me," he continued, "you immediately entered my world, and at that moment your friends no longer remembered that you had even seen the UFO, called out, or come running over here. They continued to see you as you were on

119

the toboggan, just before the UFO became visible to you; and when you return, they will not even be aware that you ever left."

He paused again and looked at the three who stood before him, trying to understand. "You see, in the past when you came to my world you first had to leave your own and then, moving between time, come into ours. When you returned home, you found your time had not altered. But now that you three have become *true citizens,* you can be in both worlds, doing different things at the same time. Do you understand, even a little?"

"No, but I'm not going to worry about it," said Bill with a smile. "You say we are 'true citizens'—does that mean we're safe now from the Dark Ones?"

"Only if you don't attempt to wander about alone without shields and a supply of white stones. If you obey our rules and remember the secret, the Dark Ones have no power over you. You may visit us as often as you wish. There is much to see and learn." He smiled at them, his silver-blue eyes twinkling with delight.

"After tonight you will, of course, come and go in your own 'saucers,' as you call them. They will be yours forever."

"That will be just—just *super!*" exclaimed Bill, completely at a loss for the right words. "But," he added, "what *is* the secret? What did we learn?"

"Yes," said Lily. "How did *I* get to come?"

"I didn't do anything," declared Harold. "I don't get it."

Promise-Keeper looked at Harold.

"You're only young," he said, "but you always believed I would keep my word. That is enough for citizenship. There are also rewards."

He turned to Lily.

"What color is your best dress, Lily?"

"Green," she said. "It was going to be blue, but—" She stopped suddenly, looked down at her feet.

"That's right." Promise-Keeper smiled.

"And me? What about me?" asked Bill.

Promise-Keeper answered not a word, but his silver-blue eyes rested for a second on the terrible scarf.

Bill, understanding, looked back at the others, now preparing to swoop down the hill.

"Can they become citizens too?" he asked.

"They have made a start," said Promise-Keeper, "and that is the only way to get anywhere." He looked then at the silver craft. "If we four are ever to get to the valley," he added, "we had best be on our way. Please shut your eyes and keep them shut until I tell you to open them."

They did as he said and, as before, felt the ground slip away from beneath their feet. When they were allowed to open their eyes they discovered they were once more in the silver UFO, on their way to the world beyond the stars.

But this time as true citizens. Owning their own saucers, protected by the white shields of Abilan and the strange white stones, they would be able to come and go as they pleased—for ever and ever! And the Dark Ones would not be able to drive them out or make them forget where they had been.

Promise-Keeper had said so, and they knew that his word could not be broken.